This Isn't
SHAKESPEARE

This Isn't
Shakespeare

a novel

STEPHANIE CARDEL

WordCrafts Press

This Isn't Shakespeare
Copyright © 2025
Stephanie Cardel

Hardback ISBN: 978-1-967649-22-8
Paperback ISBN: 978-1-967649-23-5

Cover concept and design by Anna Hester.

Published by WordCrafts Press
Cody, Wyoming 82414
www.wordcrafts.net

For all who've sinned and fall short of the glory of God.
He sees you. He loves you. He can forgive you.

Finally, brothers and sisters, whatever is true, whatever is noble, whatever is right, whatever is pure, whatever is lovely, whatever is admirable—if anything is excellent or praiseworthy—think about such things.

~Philippians 4:8

Chapter One

We sit on the warm hood of my green Taurus in Cal's driveway and gaze at the endless summer sky. My back rests against his chest, but my heart sticks in my throat when I remember it's our last night together. We watch the heavens fade to black, a darkness that could swallow us whole if gravity reversed. I feel like it *will* reverse when he leaves for college tomorrow.

"Doubt thou the stars are fire; Doubt that the sun doth move; doubt truth to be a liar; But never doubt I love," I say.

Cal wraps his arms around me. "What's that one from?"

"A love letter by Hamlet." Shakespeare always has a quote that speaks my heart.

Twenty-one days before I see Cal again. He'll be four long hours away.

Maybe it wouldn't seem so awful if we hadn't spent every spare minute together since we made up in July. At least we can text and call now. He hasn't had a phone since he lost his before we got back together, so we went and got one today with a prepaid plan. I paid for the first three months and covered all the fees as a going away gift.

But senior year is still looking bleak.

I can't think about that, though. I can't even imagine it. I close my eyes against the tears and focus on right now. My body rises and falls as Cal breathes, and I lose myself in the perfectness of being here in this moment, his heat flooding my back. A moment that tastes of forever and happily-ever-after. Then I ruin it.

"How can you look at that sky and not believe in God?"

He twirls a strand of my long brown hair around his finger. "Madison…" There's a tiny warning there. He won't be dragged into that conversation again.

The reminder starts to crimp the edges of the perfectness.

Before the frown has time to fully form on my face, he presses his cheek to mine and hums the old Journey song that was playing when we met. A peace offering. I relax back into him and smile. We are completely in sync in so many other ways. He kisses my shoulder, and the moment is all poetic again.

Then *he* ruins it by slipping his hands beneath my shirt.

"Please," he says softly. "It'll be like a going-away present."

I place his hands back on top of my shirt. "I already got you a present."

He nuzzles my neck. "That phone is as much for you as it is for me."

"So you're saying sex would be just for you. Wow. How can I resist?"

His deep laugh is soft and sexy in my ear. "You know you want to."

I sigh, which he must think means I'm into it, because he steps up his efforts. I sit up straight, stopping him cold. "Cal—" Now I've got the warning tone.

He pulls me back to his chest. "You're right. I'm sorry. You can't blame a guy for trying. I love you, Mads."

I'm glad I can't see his eyes right now. Those blue eyes hold such power over me. He knows it too. I'm close to giving in. And it's not that I don't want to.

It just seems so. . .sacred.

My bestie, Sophie, and I agreed to support each other in the face of the world on this. Having her in my corner helps me stand firm against Cal's pressure.

"Let's go get something to eat. I'm starving," he says.

"Already? We just ate an hour ago." But I'm thankful for the subject change.

"Yeah, but we split that sub, and I could've eaten the whole thing." He kisses up and down my neck until I giggle. "All of my appetites are voracious," he whispers.

"I'll just wait out here."

"Come on. I told you, my old man's in his room," he says, reading my mind. "We won't even see him." He slides us both off the car, and we walk into the dark, quiet house to the kitchen. The old fluorescent light buzzes softly over a sink overflowing with dirty dishes. An open bottle of Scotch sits on the counter. My stomach tightens in a knot.

"Will you make me a sandwich? I'll go make sure he's out for the night and isn't going to bother us." Cal stops in the doorway. "Remember, mayo on the cheese side…"

"Mustard on the bologna side, I know," I finish. He's so picky about his condiments. I want to wash the dishes, but I grab a paper plate from the pantry instead. I won't spend my last night with Cal cleaning his father's kitchen. I hum as I make the sandwich and imagine making his lunch for him to take to work someday, tucking a love note in the sandwich bag like I've seen my mom do.

Loud shouts and swearing break into my daydream. My heart speeds up. I press the knife hard into the sandwich to stop my shaking hands. *I hate this so much.* Which is why I wanted to stay outside. Drinking and the Westfall men don't mix. I hum a little louder.

When he comes back, he gets a beer to go with his sandwich. I give him a disgusted look.

"What? I'm not going to be driving."

That's not the point, but I let it drop. I know one beer is not a big deal. It's just that it's only been a week since the end of summer party at Joey's, and I never want to see him like that again.

"I should probably go home," I say. "I haven't done my barre exercises in three nights. You're a bad influence." I nudge him playfully with my shoulder.

"You can't leave now. It's only 9:00. I don't get why you kill yourself training anyway. It's not like you're going to Julliard. You aren't even going to major in dance next year."

"Your school doesn't have a dance major." *Which is why I'm not sure I should go there.*

"Exactly. So cut yourself some slack."

The words, *I want to be a professional dancer,* get stuck somewhere between my heart and my mouth. He would freak if he knew I'm even considering not following him to school next year.

Tonight is not the night to bring it up.

"I have a Shakespeare quote for your leaving," I say instead.

"Of course, you do. Let's hear it." His tone means he's totally humoring me.

I clear my throat. "Absence from those we love is self from self—a deadly banishment."

He grins. "Shakespeare really knows how to be miserable."

I hit his arm lightly with the back of my hand.

"Well, it is rather melodramatic, don't you think?"

"Most love poetry is." Couldn't he just let me have my gushy moment? "Are you finished?"

"Yes. It was wonderful." He wipes his mouth with his napkin. "Thank you." He kisses the back of my hand. "How about we watch a movie, my beautiful, hopeless romantic? You pick one." His blue eyes sparkle with laughter and love as they peek out from under his long, black bangs. It makes me feel all gooey inside.

I can never stay mad at him.

When he showed up at dance team camp this summer with a single red rose and an apology, I melted. I didn't even know that he knew about camp, or where it was, or when it was. So he had to have called around and found out all of this information just to surprise me. It blew me away. I couldn't help but forgive him for dumping me five months before.

Plus, he seemed genuinely sorry and said he just wasn't ready to admit that he loved me back then, and now he is. Everyone on dance team cheered when I said that I'd take him back, like it was a proposal or something. He dipped me and kissed me. It was so romantic. I get good chills every time I think about it.

The movie is almost over when Mr. Westfall opens Cal's bedroom door without knocking and then just stands there staring at us. We're sharing a gaming chair, so I feel Cal's whole body tense.

"Just ignore him," Cal says really low.

Not possible. A glaring six-three, two-hundred-and-forty-pound person is not something that I can ignore. I squeeze Cal's hand and try to swallow back my fear. *It's okay. This is Cal's dad. He won't hurt us.*

His father's glare turns to the phone that I got for Cal on his dresser. "Did your useless mother get you a cell phone anyway? After we agreed you should pay for it since you lost yours? Or did you finally get a job?" His words are slurred and way too loud for the small room.

"No, Dad, Madison gave me that." I shiver when Cal leaves the chair to go to the door. He pushes it like he's going to shut it in his dad's face. "I thought you were going to leave us alone."

"I had to make sure you weren't in here knocking her up. That's all we need."

Cal pushes the door a little farther. "We're watching a movie. Like I said. So go."

"This is my house, and I'll go when I want."

They stare at each other for a long minute with those matching eyes. I think Cal is about two seconds from forcing the door shut, so I stand up. Their attention shifts to me, and I want to sink into the floor. "Maybe I should go. It's late." I look around for my purse but feel paralyzed by the tension that has thickened the air.

"At least stay for the end of the movie," Cal says, his face pleading. If I leave, he loses the standoff. I look at his dad's angry face. He's so big. He could really hurt Cal. Would he? I never thought Cal could hurt me either, but he did when he was drunk.

I sit on the edge of the bed. "Okay." Maybe my being here helps.

"Fine. But leave the door open."

Mr. Westfall pushes the door back at Cal then retreats to the kitchen.

Cal takes my hand and pulls me up to stand close to him. "Sorry."

It's in these vulnerable moments that I love him most. I kiss him gently. "It's not your fault. A little more than kin, and less than kind."

He smiles at the quote and kisses my forehead then closes the door, and we finish watching the movie. I have no idea how it ends because the whole time I'm waiting for his father to come bursting back in.

Chapter Two

*T*hree days into our separation and I have never felt so lonely. Text messages are a poor substitute for dates. Although, Cal is texting me a lot. More than he did when we dated the first time. He's feeling lonely too.

Days of absence sad and dreary, clothed in sorrow's dark array.
Days of absence I am weary, She (He) I love is far away.

I print out the Shakespeare quote to add to the others on the wall behind the ballet barre my dad put in my room for me, along with a full-length mirror. Then I begin my workout. I go over to my barre and do some pliés to warm up, then put each leg up, stretching and arching my back. I spend the next hour, as I do every night, going through the barre exercises I did in class in the summer. I try to do at least an hour of barre work every night.

Dance team on Tuesdays and Thursdays is a great physical workout, but I need real training: forcing my body into the unnatural positions required in ballet, keeping the muscles required to do that toned. At the summer Ballet Intensive at City Ballet, I was a little behind the other dancers my age. By the end of the brutal six weeks, I had caught up—mostly. I wasn't the best in the class, but I wasn't the worst anymore. I can't let myself slide. I won't.

My phone rings before I'm finished. I assume it's Sophie, but I'm surprised to find it's Cal.

"Hi Beautiful," he says. "How's it going?"

"Good. Just working out. Everything okay?" It's so unusual for him to call.

"Just needed to hear your voice." My heart melts. I needed to hear his voice too.

We talk for about ten minutes. He sounds miserable. I wish

I could reach through the phone and give him a hug. I miss his arms around me.

I call Sophie the next day to talk. School starts tomorrow, and we need to coordinate. For the first time in five years her family's annual trip to the lake didn't include me. I didn't really miss it since I was with Cal, but it feels a little weird starting school already when I didn't go. Her super strict parents actually let her boyfriend Tim go in my place.

"So how'd it go?" I ask her.

"Ugh. They didn't give us a minute of privacy. Not one. If they weren't with us, they made my little brother go with us."

I'm not surprised, but best friends must be sympathetic. "Bummer." I've only experienced *her* parents' over-protectiveness. Mine were like, "Yay, she's got her license. We don't have to drive her around anymore." So, I'm alone in the house a lot, like now. My parents give me unlimited privacy, and my older sister is already married with a baby. I prop my feet on the arm of the couch, in spite of how my mom feels about it, because I can.

Then I cave and put my feet back on the floor.

I'm a terrible rebel.

I've never been bold and confident like Sophie or like my sister Kayleigh. Of course, why wouldn't they be? They excel at everything they do. Kayleigh was first chair violin in the orchestra, debate club president, a cheerleader, and homecoming queen. Sophie is flag captain, won the state science fair, in the Honor Society, and she'll probably be valedictorian.

I bombed orchestra auditions, had to run off stage and puke during my first and last debate, and I'm a solid "B" student. The only thing I've ever been good at is dance.

And being Cal's girlfriend. I am an excellent girlfriend. I'm all in this time.

"How does your beloved pompous pinhead like college life so far?" Sophie asks to be nice. For her. Not a fan of Cal.

"He doesn't have any friends yet, so he's kind of lonely."

"Should've gone somewhere closer and commuted."

"And pass up a full scholarship? Plus, they have a great pre-med program. Even if he had stayed closer to home, he wouldn't have had the gas money to drive back and forth."

"The lazy bum should've thought of that this summer when the rest of us were working our tails off. Anyway, you would've driven to see him—probably every night."

"He couldn't find a job at first, then he didn't want to get one he was going to have to quit so soon." I repeat the same excuses he gave me. They sound just as empty. Most employers are willing to accommodate college students by giving them a few hours when they get to come home on weekends and breaks, and we all know it.

"Riiiight. New topic. What are you wearing tomorrow?"

Our discussion turns to clothes (my new blue mini dress with leggings) and shoes (my blue sandals with the rhinestones) and when we will meet and where (in front of the band room at 7:45) and whether or not we'll share lockers again. (Yes, definitely. One for coats and other junk we don't want to lug around and one for our books.)

"Are you going to the ballet with your dad tonight?" she asks.

"Yep. I can't wait!"

She laughs. "Can you imagine my dad taking me to the ballet? Our parents are polar opposites."

I laugh too, but really, even though her parents don't love the ballet, they would have front row seats if she was performing. They used to come to all three of our recitals each year. They would support her one hundred percent if she wanted to be a professional ballet dancer. My parents…well, they're too worried about what's practical.

If it be thus to dream, still let me sleep.

The dancers slowly merge into a final pose, all connected, but maintaining their individuality at the same time. A perfect ending to an amazing performance. My arms tingle with goose bumps as the orchestra plays the last note. I jump from my seat, clapping, my heart racing, my eyes tearing up just a bit.

Others stand here and there as the dancers take their bows. Eventually, my dad stands next to me. His claps are slow and steady, not like my rapid, enthusiastic ones that are making my hands hurt.

I feel his eyes on me instead of the stage, so I turn to him. "Amazing, right?"

"Almost as good as you." He touches the end of my nose.

I roll my eyes and shake my head and sigh. Always my biggest fan.

"I need a pit stop," he says, "so I'll meet you in the lobby."

I nod and gather my program and my purse as he exits the aisle. He got us really good seats—tenth row, center. Maybe because it's our last daddy-daughter-before-school-starts date. My sister is five years older, so he started the tradition with her when she hit high school, then it was my turn. I can't believe it's the last one.

I walk over to the display about the dancers. I glance at the short bios about each one. I already read them in the program, but there are a handful of different dancers here that seem pretty young. It says they're all in Company Two. I didn't know that was a thing. I thought they only had the main company that performed tonight.

There's a pocket with brochures about City Ballet auditions. I snatch one.

This is it. This is what I've been searching for. Company Two is a part-time company for college students. It's an actual paid professional company but allows the members to be enrolled in a program at Bellmeade College. I can be a professional dancer *and* appease my parents. Tryouts are in May. Hope blooms in my chest.

I jump when my dad touches my arm.

"Whoa! Just me. You ready to go?"

"Sorry. Yeah." I grab another brochure about classes and shove them both into my purse.

By the time we get to the car that blooming hope has turned into a big wad of sadness sitting in my stomach. First of all, they don't just want me to go to college. Mom is expecting me to be a teacher, like her. Second, I'm probably not good enough. And my parents aren't going to pay for more classes. Third, my heart chimes in, *what about Calvin?*

When we get home, I shower and get settled in my PJs, ready

to curl up to finish the sweet romance I've been reading, since assigned reading will take over my reading time next week. I hear a commotion upstairs like someone is coming in the back door. Who in the world would come over so late? I thought my parents were already in bed.

I dash up the stairs to find my sister. Her eyes are red and puffy with mascara rings under them. My precious niece is asleep in her arms.

"Can you take her so I can set up the play pen in my old room?" she asks. Her voice is strained with emotion. Mom and Dad come down the hall, both trying to wrestle on their robes.

I take little Kaitlyn and her diaper bag. Kayleigh goes to get more stuff from her car.

"What's going on?" Mom asks.

Kayleigh looks over her shoulder and mumbles, "I need to stay here tonight, okay?" The screen door closes on the last word. Mom looks at me and I shrug. Dad follows Kayleigh out to help.

Mom crosses her arms. "They must've had a fight." She raises her eyebrows, and I can practically read her thoughts: *I told you so*.

And the fourth reason I can't be a professional dancer: Against my parents' wishes, Kayleigh didn't finish college before she got married. Kayleigh had a baby right away. I'm supposed to be *smarter than that*.

Chapter Three

There's a slight drizzle Wednesday morning which we didn't expect when we decided to meet outside. Always punctual Sophie waves from under the cafeteria door awning. I put my notebook over my head and dash to her. Tim is zoned to a different high school, which saves me from being a third wheel. It was so awkward when I would hang out with them at the beginning of the summer before Cal and I got back together.

Sophie is my opposite in just about every way possible: blonde curly hair, dark eyes, a head shorter, and a curvy figure. I'm tall and too skinny to have any curves. She's wearing a melon-colored top that looks great with her dark summer tan and low-rise jeans that accentuate those curves.

"That's not what you said you were wearing, but I like it," I say.

She frowns at me as we go into the building. "I still can't believe you are deserting me our *senior* year. This was supposed to be the best year ever."

And she says I'm melodramatic. "I'm not deserting you. We'll see each other every morning in homeroom, and we'll have English together before I leave for work."

"Yeah, big whoop. How can you drop marching band our *senior* year? It's sacrilegious!"

"You know I can't do band and dance team. They practice at the same time."

"But the band has been your family for three years. You didn't have to join the dance team just because Miss Gena left us."

"I needed to keep training somehow. Besides, I stink at the clarinet. The only reason Mr. Marley kept me around was because I could learn the flag routines—because of dance."

"Whatever." She runs her hand along the strap of her backpack on her shoulder. "I could kill Miss Gena for running off and getting married and closing her studio our *senior* year. We gave eight years of our lives to that woman."

I laugh. "I think it's the other way around. It's about time she got married. And would you stop saying 'our *senior* year' like that?"

"You're still deserting me. Who am I going to sit with on the bus at away games and competitions?"

"Who did you sit with last year? It wasn't me. Half the time, I ended up with Robert Kessler." He's a loner by choice. My sitting with him just so I'd have someone to talk to made me take a few hits to my already sub-par social status. "You have tons of other friends, and you know it." I'm the lonely one in this duet. "Stop whining."

She sticks her tongue out at me and then grins. "Yes, Mom. I think Robert developed quite a crush. He's been asking about you."

Great. Robert comes up to my chin and has serious sinus issues. Okay, maybe he's not a loner by choice.

We get to Mrs. Evers' homeroom class and take seats in the second row. Before I get a chance to calm her fears of desertion by asking her to come spend the night this weekend, Mrs. Evers announces, "The seating chart is on the board."

A collective moan comes from the class just as the first bell rings. It's alphabetical, so Sophie Applegate is in the first seat, and I, Madison Ragland, am in the middle of the third row. We roll our eyes at each other, but short of lip reading, we'll have to get to school every day in time to talk before homeroom. Considering I'm not a morning person, I don't see that happening. As I get settled in the new seat, Mrs. Evers calls my name.

"Madison, since you'll be in my first period class and won't need to rush out, would you mark the roll each day for me immediately after the announcements?" I had Mrs. Evers for Early Childhood Education II last year. She's nice, just, kind of a perfectionist sometimes. I'm used to that, though, because of my mom.

"Yes, ma'am."

"Teacher's pet," Ken Reynolds hisses as he slides into the seat behind me as the final bell rings. I fake-scowl at him, then smile, which he returns. I feel all fluttery inside and have to turn back around to keep from melting down. Ken Reynolds—the football player, the class vice president, the guy voted best looking for three years running just—Smiled. At. Me. I glance over at Sophie and her eyebrows lift. She saw it too. Ken Reynolds doesn't smile at band geeks like me.

The television mounted in the corner of the room comes on and everyone stands up. The words of the pledge of allegiance appear over a waving flag as the national anthem plays.

I consider the smile.

Number one, it doesn't matter how hot he is, I have a boyfriend. Number two, he has a girlfriend who is on the dance team, so it's possible that he has seen me at practice and no longer considers me a band geek. Number three, it was just a smile for heaven's sake, and I'm blowing it way out of proportion. *Breathe, Madison. Stop being such a geek.*

A mixture of excitement and fear battles inside me as I think about the fact that Ken Reynolds—The Kenneth Reynolds—will be sitting behind me at the beginning of every day this year. It's like meeting a celebrity. I'm so awkward. How will I even speak to him? Sometimes I wish I was more like Sophie. She always has a sassy comeback.

I refuse to be afraid. It is our *senior* year after all, and I already have a wonderful boyfriend who loves me. What's wrong with a little harmless flirting? Especially if it means I get to see Kenneth Reynolds' swoon-worthy smile.

Everyone sits when our class president, David Taylor, comes on the screen to give the announcements. Mrs. Evers hands out our locker assignments when I go up to her desk and take the roll. Ken's hazel eyes—so striking against his dark skin—look me up and down as I walk back to my seat, and I feel my face flush.

He leans over his desk so that his lips are close to my ear. "Mmmhmm, I wouldn't mind taking a roll with you, if you know what I mean."

Crude. But…Ken Reynolds is flirting with me?
What would Sophie say?

She would be bold. Sassy. Disdainful.

I turn around with a grin, arch an eyebrow and give *him* a once over. "Get over yourself. I have a boyfriend."

The bell rings, and he grabs his backpack and stands. "Lucky guy," he says as he dazzles me with another smile.

"What the heck?" Sophie rushes over before I even start breathing again. "What was all that?"

"I know. Right?" My face heats again, embarrassed that I even talked to him.

"Maybe I was wrong about you getting back together with Calvin," she says. "You seem different." She looks at me suspiciously. "Where's all this…confidence coming from?"

"I pretended I was you," I admit.

She laughs. "Well, I like it. Keep it up. What's your locker number? I gotta go." She looks at the forgotten slip of paper on my desk. "Crud. They aren't even on the same hall." She walks away but turns at the door. "See if you can switch with someone. Mine's near English."

The others file in for Teaching as a Profession or TAP with Mrs. Evers. It's required in my career path laid out for me in eighth grade when I thought I wanted to be an elementary school teacher like my mom. If it's anything like Early Childhood Education, it will be a breeze. I love kids—especially teaching them dance—and helping my mom at her school has taught me a lot already. Teaching school is a good fit for me.

But dance…is my passion. To dance as my job? The dream.

I worked my tutu off my sophomore and junior years, so I could breeze through this year. I've got to suffer through Pre-Calculus after this, but then it's Cooperative Education, which is basically elementary marketing—so easy, but it allows me to leave after AP English and go to work. Mostly, non-college bound people take C.E. for trade school training, but any job is allowed and since my mom has mentored me for the past three years, I told her I just wanted to earn money not volunteer at her school. She was not happy.

It's the first time I purposely disappointed my mom. How can I break her heart and tell her I don't want to be a teacher on top of that? My sister already broke Mom's heart by dropping out of college.

My plan was to take C.E. so I'd be out of school early enough to go to dance classes in Nashville every night—not that I told Mom that. But then I was elected dance team captain, and Cal and I got back together, so my plan got a little fuzzy.

Really fuzzy.

After going to the ballet and learning about Company Two, it feels like it's coming back in focus. I researched the program at Bellmeade College last night. It offers college credit for just being a City Ballet Company Two member. It's their second-string company, but it's still a real, full-time professional company. The dancers get paid to be in it and can go to school part-time on nights and weekends. The college lets you choose a major or design your own Liberal Arts major with a focus on dance—getting credit for being in the company. And they give huge tuition discounts because dancers don't make much money. It's the best of both worlds. My dream come true.

Except, where would Calvin fit into that?

Bellmeade is a private Christian college. They have a good Biology program and a good pre-med program too, but they require that students attend chapel. There's no way Calvin would consider transferring to a Christian college. No way—even if his parents would pay for it—which they wouldn't. So if I go to school in Nashville, where I'll have company rehearsals all day every day and classes and studying all evening, and Cal stays in Knoxville with his tough Biology major, it basically means giving up Cal for dance. We'd never see each other.

Isn't love more important than career choice? And what if I'm not even good enough to make it into the company?

Everyone assumes that I'm going to school with Calvin and majoring in Education. That's the sensible thing to do, and I'm the sensible one, the responsible one, the one everyone's parents know they can count on, the teacher's pet. Practically perfect in every way. I shudder at the thought.

"Are you cold?" Kendra, a friend that goes to my church, asks. She holds out a sweater and sits down in the seat in front of me.

"No thanks, I'm okay."

She puts the sweater on the back of her chair. "You never know about the temperature in this place. I always like to be prepared," she says. "I've missed you at youth group lately."

"I was spending as much time as I could with my boyfriend before he went away to school. But I'm going tonight."

Her face brightens. "Is there any way you could give me a ride? Kevin has to work."

"Sure. No problem."

"I hope you like where you're sitting," Mrs. Evers says. "It's officially your assigned seat." She begins writing down everyone's names on the seating chart while someone hands out the books, and I try to tear my thoughts from the hazy future that has me tied up in knots.

Pre-Calculus is a nightmare, and C.E. is boring as all get out, but finally, I take my seat next to Sophie in AP English. I know this class will not be easy, but at least the first semester we'll be studying poetry. And with a whole section on Shakespeare!

"This is going to be great," I whisper to Sophie while Dr. Northcutt finishes handing out the syllabi.

She rolls her eyes and makes a gagging motion with her finger.

I just grin at her.

She shakes her head like I'm a lost cause. "I'm counting on your mad poetry skills to get me through this."

"Only if you promise to get me through Pre-Calculus."

"Done."

Sophie and I complement each other well, and even though we don't exactly see eye-to-eye on a lot of things, we've got each other's back. Her strict parents have inspired her to be a bit more rebellious than me. I've had to rescue her from parties and be her cover story more times than I'd like to remember. But that's what you do for your bestie. She wasn't thrilled that I got back together with Calvin. But she'd be the first to defend that choice to someone else.

The way I see it, life boils down to choices. You make good choices, you stick to your commitments, you trust in God to guide you, and you have a good life. I don't look down my nose at her choices—whether I agree with them or not. She has a right to live her life as she sees fit, and I choose to love her, whatever that looks like.

A friend is one that knows you as you are, understands where you have been, accepts what you have become, and still, gently allows you to grow.

Well said, William.

I just wish Shakespeare had some advice on how to choose between the dream career and the dream guy. But no—I've looked. Crickets from Will. Crickets from God—no matter how hard I pray. It's enough to make a girl curl into a great big ball of coward.

When I get to Purple Pansy Pizza for my first weekday shift, I'm starving. So is everyone else in town if the line out of the door is any indication. The manager, Abdulla, tells me to hurry and change into my uniform. My friend Laurie, who's in my C.E. class, is already in the bathroom.

"I didn't even think about bringing a lunch. The pizza smells so good, it's killing me," I say as I lock myself in a stall.

"I know. And it'll be forever before we get a break. I'm definitely bringing a snack tomorrow." She breezes out, and I finish dressing and pull my hair into a ponytail as fast as I can.

After I shove my stuff in a cubby in the kitchen, I turn on my hostess charm and hustle drinks, salads, and pizza for the next two hours without stopping. Once the rush is over, I remember how hungry I am. Laurie gets to leave. She'll work 12:00–2:00 on Mondays, Wednesdays, and every other Friday while I work 12:00–4:30. We'll switch on Tuesdays and Thursdays so I can go to dance team practice. She buys a Coke on her way out, and I stare at it like I've been stranded on a desert island as I hand it over. Pity makes her offer me a sip. The small rush of sugar helps restore my strength a tiny bit. But I'll need more fortification.

I don't see Abdulla anywhere, and the blinds are closed on his office, so I go where counter girls are forbidden: where they make the pizzas.

Rick and Scott aren't there even though they've been passing pizzas to me for the past two hours. I've only seen the new guy from the back and don't even know his name, but desperation causes me to beg, "If you give me a mushroom, you'll save my life."

"Why would I want to do that?" He turns around, and I draw in a breath. It's Nathan Ford. A bigger, broader, hotter Nathan Ford than the one that I cheated on in ninth grade, but definitely him.

It feels like I've been punched in the gut.

Chapter Four

I can't think. I can't move. My eyes are probably bugging out of my head.

"Relax Madison, I'm just kidding." Nathan hands me a couple of mushrooms.

I'm just staring at them with my mouth hanging open like a fish on the sand. It's a few infinite seconds before I can breathe again. "I, uh, didn't know it was you." I stammer out a thank-you and rush to the kitchen to get a busing tray. I shove the mushrooms in my mouth before I push through the door and run straight into Abdulla.

"Did you meet the new guy?" he asks me. He has a pretty thick accent, since he grew up in Saudi Arabia. Luckily, I can usually understand him.

I swallow the mushrooms whole, so I won't get in trouble. "Yeah. We already know each other," I answer. *And he hates me.*

"Good. You can show him how to handle the counter. He's doing pretty good. He has that C.E. thing like you and Laurie."

He makes it sound like a condition. I just nod, desperate to get away in case the tears I feel threatening actually come. Thankfully, he sees a customer he knows and goes over to talk to him. I start throwing plates and cups into the tub, but all I can see is Nathan's angry, hurt face as he calls me a two-timing witch in front of the whole ninth grade.

It was the worst thing I've ever done. The worst choice I've ever made. I'll never forgive myself, so I can't imagine he'll ever forgive me. My hands are shaking so much as I try to wipe down the table that Abdulla notices.

"What is wrong with you?" he asks me, his face all crinkled up with disgust.

"I, uh, I'm just really hungry. My blood sugar is low."

"Well, take your fifteen and eat something." He takes the tray out of my hands and starts mumbling under his breath as he carries it back to the kitchen. I sit in the empty booth for a minute to compose myself. But it's like trying to stop a flood with a bucket.

All those memories I'd pushed so deep inside wash over me. That night is seared on my brain.

The quickest thing to eat is a pre-prepared salad, so I grab one from the refrigerator and pay for it. I sit in a booth in the far back corner of the restaurant wishing I could just disappear or at least go home. I don't know how I'm going to face him. We haven't even spoken since that day. Not that I spoke. I just cried. The next three months of seeing those angry brown eyes in the halls at school every day were torture. I practically stopped breathing whenever I caught a glimpse of any guy with a similar mop of dark blond hair. I can barely breathe now.

"I'm starving too. Can I sit with you?" Nathan slides in across from me without waiting for my answer. I look up at him with wide eyes and swallow hard, the tears threatening again.

"Things aren't going to be weird between us, are they?" he asks, taking off his Purple Pansy hat and setting it on the seat. His hair is much shorter than he used to wear it, and darker, although it's got some highlights, probably from the summer sun.

I shake my head, but the stupid tears start leaking out of my eyes.

"Why are you crying?" He's looking at me like I'm nuts.

I stare at the table. The words I never had the chance to say pour out of me like hot lava, burning my throat. "I didn't even like him. Sophie couldn't go out with Caleb unless we doubled, and he had a car, and a license, and I thought I'd just go and be nice, but tell him I had a boyfriend, and I wasn't interested, you know, but he just assumed, and he was older and more experienced and the next thing I knew, we were at the theatre, and he pulled me into his lap and started kissing me, and I didn't know what to do, and I pushed him away and ran to the bathroom, but I saw Keith in the back row as I ran out, and I knew he'd tell you, and I knew you'd hate me, and I'd screwed up so bad that there was no way to fix it. So

I just didn't even try at all, and I made the worst choice ever and just went back to my seat and pretended that everything was okay when inside I was so, so sorry and …" I'm bawling by this point. I don't even know if he can understand me.

"Good grief Maddy, breathe. It's okay. It was a long time ago."

I can't look at him. I stare at my salad. The burning, bubbling lava settling in my stomach takes away my appetite. I wipe my eyes and hear him chuckle. "I can't believe you've been holding all that inside you all this time."

I draw in a ragged breath of thick, guilty air. "You don't hate me?"

"I never hated you. I was hurt and angry, and I was sorry I yelled at you in front of everyone, but I never hated you."

I dare to look at him. I don't believe it. "You have nothing to be sorry for. I've always felt so awful about it."

"Geez. Let it go. I forgave you a long time ago." Forgiveness is worse than hatred. I bury my face in my hands. Hatred is what I deserve. The fact that he forgave me a long time ago just proves how nice he is, and how awful I am for making such a terrible choice. I really, really liked him. Maybe even loved him. I still don't know why I did it and still wish I never had.

"You aren't going to have time to finish that salad. I've got five minutes, but your time is up." He pauses, but I don't respond. "If it will make you feel better, I'll let you give me your salad. We'll call it a peace offering."

Somehow that makes me smile. "Fine. Take it." I push it to him.

"We good?" he asks.

"Sure," I lie. How could we ever be good? I know those eyes, and they're guarded. He's lying too.

I go to the bathroom and try to repair the damage my crying did. It makes me late coming back from my break. I can't believe how relieved I feel to have finally told Nathan my side of the story. I mean, I was wrong all the way around, but I never apologized, never had a chance to explain that I didn't want it to happen and had never wanted to hurt him. I was just a stupid, unprepared, fourteen-year-old *infant* who had no business being on a date with a sixteen-year-old in the first place. Why did my parents let me do that?

Not that my intentions matter. It's my actions that matter. That's why ever since then I've been so careful about my choices. I never want to feel regret like that again. And I never want my choices to cause someone else pain.

"You're late and you look awful. What have you been doing?" Abdulla asks, narrowing his black eyes at me.

It's obvious I've been crying, so I say, "I'm fine. Thanks for caring." I couldn't get away with the attitude if I was talking to Mr. Boyd, the owner, but Abdulla treats us more like friends than employees. A customer comes in, so I'm spared further conversation.

As I walk past Abdulla to the register, he mutters, "Drama queen."

I guess I am that. Today anyway. Freaking out because Ken Reynolds smiled at me earlier and now having a total meltdown over something that happened three years ago. Ridiculous. I take a deep breath. I'll blame it on hormones.

Nathan comes back from his break just as I finish up with the customer. "Abdulla said you're supposed to teach me how to handle the counter. What's up with that anyway? Girls aren't allowed to make the pizzas, but boys are allowed to work the counter?"

I take a deep breath. If he can pretend, so can I.

"Boys aren't supposed to work the counter. It's only if, like now, there's only one girl here, and I have to go to the bathroom or something. Mr. Boyd says he prefers female waitresses. I suppose someone could file a lawsuit."

"I kind of see his point."

"You do? I never pegged you for a sexist."

"I'm not. I just hate it when I get a male waiter at a restaurant."

I narrow my eyes at him. "Why?"

He shrugs. "I don't know. I just do. Maybe because I know how disgusting guys are."

I show him where everything is and how to operate the cash register, how much ice to put in the cups, how we have to use the scooper and not the cup so it doesn't scrape wax into the drink, how we have to pour the excess moisture out of the salads before we serve them, all the stuff that has become second nature to me after two years. The whole time he watches me with those sexy brown eyes and those full lips slightly turned up on the edges like he's amused, and I dare to wonder if he's thinking about the same thing I am, about what was possibly the greatest first kiss in the history of the world.

That magical kiss happened at a different pizza place on the other side of town. Everybody was there because it was Friday night and that's where all the cool freshman from Benjamin Franklin High hung out after the football games. Back then, us band geeks didn't know we weren't cool.

My mom had just texted me that she was waiting in the parking lot, so I had to go. She didn't know I had a boyfriend, and I didn't want her to. I slid out of the booth, and he stood too, our hands still joined.

All of our friends started chanting, "Kiss! Kiss! Kiss..."

I didn't want my first kiss to be on display, but when Nathan reached up and cupped his hand on my face, everyone around us just disappeared. He leaned in and brought his warm, soft lips to mine. Our warm pizza breath mingled for just a second and when our lips touched, I was transported to another place, and the only sound I heard was my heart pounding in my ears. When I opened my eyes, I realized everyone was cheering.

Truly magical. I've had lots of first kisses with guys since. None with that kind of chemistry—until Cal.

Nathan clears his throat, and I'm pulled back to the present. I've been staring at him—at his lips. My face burns.

"So, I guess you still go to Franklin," he says.

I nod and begin furiously wiping down the already perfectly clean counter. He moved the next summer and got re-zoned. He has zero social media presence—which is one of the reasons I didn't realize he was the new guy. "Where do you go?"

"I'm a Buchanan Buccaneer." He rolls his eyes. "What a lame mascot. Why would they want us to be proud of being a pirate? Aren't they all thieves and murderers?"

"It's way better than the Franklin Flames. Honestly, it's embarrassing. It's not a mascot, it's an element."

"At least you can get fired up about it." He laughs at his dumb joke.

"Since you go to Buchanan, you might know my boyfriend. Calvin Westfall?"

That first kiss was a long time ago, and even though I still think Nathan's great, I learned my lesson about cheating and drawing lines right up front.

He makes a face. "That's your boyfriend?"

"You know him?"

He nods. "I had a class with him. I don't really *know* him." He's still looking at me like he's disgusted.

"What?" I finally say.

"I just think you could do better. He seemed like a jerk. Always talking about parties and getting wasted. I didn't expect you to turn into a party girl."

"I didn't... I mean, I'm not. And he's not either, really. Not anymore." I see Abdulla enter the kitchen behind Nathan carrying a new money tray for the register. "So that's all there is to the counter," I say waving my arm at it. "During this down time before the dinner rush, we have to prep for the next shift."

Abdulla walks up to us. "I've got you both scheduled for Labor Day because you didn't ask off."

Nathan looks surprised. "I thought we'd be closed. I'm going dove hunting with my dad and grandfather."

"Not if you don't get someone to cover your shift." Abdulla gives him a sugary smile. "Good luck, Chuck. Just about everyone else asked off." He walks away to change out the register money trays.

"Great," Nathan says.

Now I'm the one with the disgusted look.

"What?" he asks.

"You like to shoot pretty little birds out of the sky?" I'm glad Cal doesn't hunt.

"Oh, brother. You aren't a member of PETA are you?"

"I've considered it," I say, lifting my chin.

He shakes his head as he walks backward toward the pizza making area. "Well then, brace yourself, because I don't just dove hunt, I deer hunt and turkey hunt too." He holds up his hands in an apologetic way at the look of horror on my face but turns and continues to walk away.

I go back to the kitchen area to wash dishes, practically hyperventilating, my eyes tearing up again. Is this how it's going to be? Pretending like we're friends every day at work? It was easy as long as I didn't think about who I was talking to but a sharp slap in the face every time I remembered.

Work was the one place I didn't have to play a part to please someone. I honestly don't know how I'm going to handle this.

I'm doing barre exercises in my room when Mom comes in with a stack of laundry. "Getting ready for *The Nutcracker* tryouts?"

"Yep."

She watches me lift my leg up beside my head. "Beautiful. You're so talented, Madison. How was your first day of senior year?"

"It was good. Busy. Pre-Calculus is going to be a challenge."

"As you know, I can't help you with that, but your dad can. I was sad that we didn't go for ice cream since you were still working when I got home. I think it's the only first day that we didn't. And it's your last first day. Maybe we can go Saturday?"

"That would be great."

She sets the laundry on my dresser and notices the City Ballet brochures. "What's this?"

Crud. I'm not ready for this discussion.

"Um, I was hoping I could talk to you about taking classes there—after *Nutcracker*."

Her face twists up, and she shakes her head. "That Intensive you took in the summer was really expensive. I'm sure their classes are too. *Nutcracker* is free. Dance team is free. I mean, there are expenses involved, but I'm relieved we don't have that monthly expense from classes anymore. There's no point in taking more classes anyway when that's not going to help you in life."

My throat feels like it's closing up. "But I really love it." I turn my back on her to hide my tears and stretch over my leg on the barre.

"I know. And you're great, but it's just a hobby. I'm sorry, honey.

We just can't pour any more money into it. Especially now, when college is right around the corner. We want to be able to pay for as much of that as we can. We don't want you starting your life in debt."

I don't respond. I can't. I hear paper crinkle and know she's wadding up the brochures and with it my hope.

Chapter Five

*T*he connected chairs feel a little claustrophobic in church today. Pastor Green's face glows like he's energized by the full house, but I'm starting to sweat. Maybe because my mind keeps wandering to the many debates Calvin and I have had about God.

The last one was the worst. I really haven't tried to talk to him about it since. We ate at this Chinese restaurant in Nashville that Cal loves and since it was such a warm, clear night we decided to walk along the riverfront. There was just enough breeze to counteract the humid August air. People buzzed all around us, walking, riding bikes and scooters, taking pictures. Music drifted to us from a bar across the street. Calvin's hand was warm and strong around mine.

"Want to go to youth group with me tomorrow night?" I asked.

He snorted with laughter. "So we can sing "Kumbaya" and make WWJD friendship bracelets?"

"It's not like that. We play volleyball and eat pizza. Then there's a lesson and prayer time."

"I'll pass."

"It's fun. And you can meet some of my friends."

He lifted our arms and twirled me around. "You're the only Jesus freak I'm interested in. I don't want to be preached to." He dipped me back and kissed me. A family with two little girls had to dodge around us. The girls giggled. I blushed.

I suppose I should have let it drop then, but I didn't. I couldn't.

"Why can't you give it a chance? I went to that laser tag place with you last week. I didn't want to, but it turned out to be fun."

"Are you seriously comparing church to laser tag?" He dropped my hand and stepped over to the railing. His knuckles went white as he gripped it. I moved beside him, watching the riverboat going by. It was decorated with lights. The people on it were laughing and talking. No awkwardness there.

The silence felt so heavy between me and Cal.

I put my hand over his. "I'm just saying you should give it a chance. I believe in God. It's an important part of who I am. I want you to share in this big, important part of me."

"God is a crutch for people who are afraid to accept that this is all there is. Christians are weak-minded, judgmental, and worst of all—hypocrites."

His words cut into my heart. "That's what you think about me?"

"No. You're different. You don't constantly throw it in my face. Usually. But look at Sophie if you want an up-close example. Her church says she's not allowed to dance or drink, but she does both. Just look at all the different ways churches try to stifle and control people. Look at how many different kinds of churches there are. It's messed up."

"Religion and faith are not the same thing. Different churches interpret theology differently. But faith is something all Christians have in common. It's believing that we're sinners in need of a Savior, and that God sent His Son to be that Savior by being the perfect and only acceptable sacrifice to put us right with God—if we believe."

He clapped his hands and closed his eyes. "I believe! I believe!" He opened his eyes. "Or do I need to click my heels three times?"

I crossed my arms and wished I could wipe that smirk off his face. "You can't dump all Christians into the hypocrite boat because you've seen some people do hypocritical things. That's like saying all Muslims are terrorists. Or all homeless people are lazy." That came out a little louder than I intended. I glanced around to see if anyone else had heard me.

"Get off your soapbox, Madison. I don't believe in God or his son, or Santa Claus for that matter. I don't need to be saved. And I don't want my girlfriend preaching sermons to me on street corners."

I'd never seen his eyes look so fierce when he was sober. "You say that's who you are," he said, "and you want to share it with me. Well, this is who I am, and you're just going to have to accept it.

And that means accepting that I don't want to share your faith or your religion with you."

I'd screwed things up. I'd hoped to ease him into the idea of coming to church with me through youth group, and instead, I hit him over the head with it.

"I'm sorry." Tears burned in my eyes. I blew it. I might've even pushed him further away from God.

Calvin put his arm around me. "I'm glad you're passionate about your faith. I'm glad you have the conviction to defend it. You're not one of the hypocrites." He kissed my head and turned me to face him, then rubbed his thumb on my cheek. "That fire in your eyes? It's so sexy." He leaned in and kissed me. "Just let this one go. Okay?"

I nodded. It was a quiet walk back to the car.

We stand to sing after the sermon. I know faith is totally a God thing. I can't change Calvin's mind, so I have to bite my tongue and agree to disagree. But what if he always feels that way? Will he ever go to church with me or be okay with my taking our kids to church? Can a marriage between two people who believe such different things be strong enough to last? The Bible says not to *yoke* yourself to a non-believer, and then goes on to say, *for what do righteousness and wickedness have in common?* That's kind of harsh. Cal's not wicked.

Still—I don't ever want to get divorced. I want to be like those old people you see that still hold hands. Like my parents who still can't wait to kiss each other when they've been apart all day. Two people, soul mates, joined forever. *Sigh.*

I wish God would give me a sign, so I would know if Calvin is really *the one.* Then I could stop obsessing over being in the dance company because my choice would take me on the other path. The one where I go to Cal's college and become a teacher. It sure would be the easier path. I wouldn't have to kill myself training on my own. I'd live up to everyone's expectations. Cal would never know that I doubted. And my mom would never know I considered breaking her heart.

It's the most important choice of my life so far. I'm afraid I'll choose wrong. If God gives me a sign, then I'll know it's right.

Everyone bows their head to pray before the Lord's Supper, but my mind is still on Cal. "Please give me a sign. Please show me what Your plan for me is. I need to know what path you want me to take. I need to know if Cal is the one." My whispered prayer is drowned out by the pastor's, but I still glance around at Kendra and my other friends to make sure no one heard.

To my surprise, Kayleigh and my brother-in-law, Derrick, come over Sunday afternoon to talk with my parents about the issues they've been having. I watch little Kaitlyn in the next room. She's just starting to pull up. Soon she'll be standing without holding on to anything. It's so cute. I lay on the floor with her and try to distract her when the voices are raised. Sometimes her little face crinkles up with worry when she hears them.

My gut twists at their angry words. That's the place I never want to be. There's a difference between arguing about something and tearing each other down with your words. I've heard my parents argue many times, but they don't fight. Not like that. I think Mom and Dad are helping, though. Showing Kayleigh and Derrick how to discuss their problems with love, reminding them who they are to each other and what's important. I'm thankful for such wise parents. Their marriage has always been a beautiful picture of real love to me.

Calvin and I argue about little things sometimes, but we never fight like that either. He doesn't purposely try to hurt me with his words, like Derrick's doing.

Except for the end of the summer party when he drank too much. But he was not himself.

We were sitting around a picnic table in Joey's backyard and Joey said, "C-man, how about we get another round and go play poker. Or better yet, we can include the girls and make it strip poker."

Calvin drained his beer. "Sounds like a plan." His words were slurred.

"I think we should go," I said. "It's getting late." I stood and tugged on his arm. He was so drunk that I think he forgot about the poker because he started to follow me.

But then Joey said, "You are so owned."

Cal didn't like that and started swearing at Joey. Things escalated fast, and my heart was hammering in my chest. But then someone made a crude joke about our lack of a sex life and everyone started laughing. Except me.

"Cal, please, can we just go?" I thought if we could slip out quickly while they were laughing, he'd forget the insult.

He tossed his empty bottle into a trash can and went for another. "No. We're going to play."

"Okay, fine, just don't drink anymore." I whispered the words.

"I'll drink as much as I want. You can't tell me what to do."

I knew it was the alcohol talking. "Then give me your keys because I'm leaving." I tried to get them from his pocket, but he turned away.

"I said we're staying." His grip on my arm got uncomfortably tight.

I jerked away from him. "I'm going." I walked toward the driveway and pulled out my cell to call Sophie. He chased after me, snatched the phone from my hand, and tossed it into the bushes beside the house.

"You'll go when I say you can." He pushed me up against the garage and tried to kiss me, but all he managed was to slobber his beer breath all over me. I would've slapped him if I could've gotten my arms loose, so instead, I kneed him in the crotch. Not hard, but he doubled over, and I went in search of my phone. I don't know if the pain sobered him up a little or what, but when I found the phone, he walked with me to the driveway.

"Don't call anyone. I'll take you home." There was no kindness in the order.

"I'm not letting *you* drive me home. You can barely walk." I pulled up Sophie's number again.

He grabbed my arm before I could hit the call button and pulled me to him. "What do you want from me, Madison?"

"I just want your keys, so I can drive us home safely." I kept walking.

He dangled the keys in front of me. "These keys? What'll you give me for 'em?" But there was no teasing quality to his voice. It was hard and cold and gave me chill bumps.

We made it to his car, and the thought of him trying to drive terrified me. He would do it if I left him. I put my phone back in my pocket.

"Please. Just give me the keys."

He backed me up to the car and left no space between us. "Begging's good." He put a hand behind my head so I couldn't lean away. "When are you gonna stop being such a tease?" He mashed his lips on mine. This time I kissed him back, hoping to calm him down.

It seemed to be working, so I put my arms around his neck and tried a different approach. "Cal, I love you. Please let me drive us home. That way you can sleep. Aren't you tired? Let me take care of you."

He slammed the keys into my chest. "Here. Drive us home—so I can sleep."

The next day I had bruises on my chest and my arm. That's when I learned he was a mean drunk just like his dad. No wonder his mom left. Calvin says his dad only started drinking heavily when he lost his job two years ago, and that he was totally different before, but I didn't know him then.

Derrick has to leave for work, and after Kayleigh has spent some time in the bathroom trying to make herself look like she hasn't been crying, she comes and joins me on the floor.

"So, tell me about Calvin," she says.

I smile. "He's tall, and handsome. He's got these awesome blue eyes. And he's really smart. He was valedictorian of his class, and he got a full scholarship in Biology. He's considering med school."

"Are you in love?" She puts her hands to her chest and bats her eyes.

I can only manage a half-smile. "That's the million-dollar question, isn't it?"

"That's not the answer I expected," she says, frowning.

"I mean, I think I am, but how do you know when a guy is really the one?"

"I guess that is the million-dollar question. If we knew a surefire way to tell, we could make a fortune matchmaking." She pokes me in the ribs then lays Kaitlyn across the bottom of her legs and lifts her up like she's flying. We both laugh as Kaitlyn giggles.

"Just remember Jeremiah 17:9," she says seriously. "The heart is deceitful above all things and beyond cure. Who can understand it?"

"I thought I was supposed to listen to my heart. What kind of awful advice is that?"

"It means that romantic love alone is not forever love, but your heart will trick you into believing it is. You have to use your head too."

My mom calls us to dinner. I'm already reeling from what Kayleigh says when she adds softly, "Just don't marry a man that doesn't support your dreams, doesn't believe in you. It wears you down until you feel like nothing." Her eyes tear up, but she turns away, picks up Kaitlyn and heads to the kitchen.

Doesn't support my dreams? Calvin doesn't even know my dreams. Why haven't I told him?

The question sits on my stomach all evening and turns my dinner into cement.

Chapter Six

Just before my shift ends, I'm rolling silverware into napkins when Nathan stands next to me and starts folding empty pizza boxes for to-go orders. "Did you find anyone to fill in for you next Monday?" I ask.

"No." His look turns sour. "My dad's really mad, too. It's a big deal family tradition, and my grandfather isn't going to be able to go for too many more years. He's starting to get some dementia."

"I'm sorry for you, but I'm glad for the birds," I say.

He sighs and shakes his head. "If it wasn't for hunting, the animals would be overpopulated. Many of them would starve to death. Doves could become as big a nuisance as pigeons or blackbirds and deer would be getting hit by cars a lot more often."

"So you think hunting is more humane?"

"Yes, I do. And you would too, if you researched the subject instead of believing the hype from the crazy bleeding hearts that are more worried about animals than humans. Besides it's good sport."

"Oh, yeah, I can see that. You, with your gun, shooting unarmed animals as they run away. Good sport."

"They may not have weapons, but that doesn't make them easy to kill. They can smell you, hear you, and see the slightest movement. And you don't want to just wound them—that would be inhumane—so you have to get it just right. It's challenging."

He looks so earnest that I have to smile. "We'll just have to agree to disagree on this topic. Let me be that I am and seek not to alter me."

He raises his eyebrows, questioning.

"Sorry. It's kind of a habit, throwing out Shakespeare quotes." I shrug and feel the blood rush to my face.

"Interesting." He seems to consider this new aspect of me for a minute. "Okay, new topic." He puts the boxes he's folded on the shelf above our heads and leans back on the counter, watching me. "What would you have been doing on Labor Day if you didn't have to work?"

"Nothing. School work. Calvin can't come home until the next weekend."

He brings me the tub that the silverware goes in. "Why not?"

"He doesn't have any extra money for gas and stuff, so he's only coming home for specific events."

He starts piling all of my rolled silverware into the big, gray tub. "And what specific event is the next weekend?"

"It's his birthday, and we're having a party."

"So he's got to save up for that. Doesn't he have a job?"

I shake my head. I don't want to mention that I'm paying for his birthday party.

"Working two jobs has its rewards. Including money for dates with Candace."

"Candace Birch?" Gorgeous. Blonde. Cheerleader.

He nods. "She goes to my church."

"What's your second job?" One job is enough for me.

"My mom's parents live at Parker House, and I work the 6:30–11:00 p.m. shift as a tech three times a week."

"Eww. You don't have to empty bedpans and stuff do you?"

"Rarely," he says, like it's nothing. "It's assisted living, so they're all pretty independent. Some have walkers or wheelchairs, but most are just a little forgetful. Besides, at that hour a lot of them are getting ready for bed."

"What do you do?" I'm horrified, fascinated, and amazed all at the same time.

"Cleaning, laundry distribution, stuff like that. Some like to play cards; some ask me to read to them. And I get to see my grandparents."

I scrape my jaw off the floor. "Wow."

"It's no big deal. Good pay too. The day techs have a lot more to do. Hard work. Even the overnighters have it worse than me with nightmares and wanderers. Sometimes it's so quiet I can do my homework."

I try to picture Calvin playing cards or reading to someone's grandpa, but I can't.

"What?" Nathan asks me.

"Nothing. I'm just impressed. How do you do it all?"

"I just have to stay on top of it."

"Do you even have any free time?"

"Sure. Like next weekend I'm going hiking with my little cousin's Cub Scout pack."

I grin. "That sounds fun, but also like work."

"No way. It's too much fun to be work."

A customer comes in and Nathan goes to the pizza making area to wait for the order. We don't talk much after that with our different prep work. The rest of the day I just keep shaking my head. Are Nathan and I actually becoming friends again?

It's raining on Labor Day, and my brain starts composing a poem for English as I'm driving to work. All through the slow day the words roll through my mind. Cal hasn't texted me since last night which is making me and the tone of the poem sad. I wonder what he's doing?

Nathan purposely bumps into my arm. "Where are you today?" He looks at me curiously.

"Just thoughtful. Working out a poem for English. We have to follow a specific rhyme scheme." I shrug and go back to wiping the counters.

"Can I hear it?"

I look sideways at him. Unsure. I don't want to be teased. Cal does enough of that. "It's not very good."

"Come on. I like your poems."

I'm about to protest that he's never read any of my poems, but I realize that's not true. I wrote him a few different love poems when we were together. And then there was the short one on the sympathy card. Still, I'm not convinced.

"You know no one else sent me a card or anything," he says.

"Well, they could just tell you how sorry they were." I couldn't.

"No one really did that either."

"It's awkward. People never know what to say at a time like that."

"You did. I still remember the verses: *Always a part of you, too young to make a start. Still here through your memory, a bookmark in your heart.* It's beautiful."

I'm so stunned, I can't respond. We were fifteen. It was a year after the break-up when his cousin died in a car accident. Nathan had been in the car too but only had minor injuries. I wanted to call him, reach out somehow, but he hated me, so I just sent a card. "I can't imagine how awful it was. I knew you were close."

"I almost called a couple of times, you know, to take you up on your offer to talk, but I chickened out."

I'm relieved. Even though I had offered to talk, what could I have said? I've never faced that kind of loss.

"I'm glad you liked it." I roll the dish towel around my hand and stare at it, so I don't have to look at him.

He puts a hand on my arm, and I feel like I've been zapped by electricity the way the warmth of it shoots through me. My head snaps up, and I have to take a step back when I see the raw hurt in his face. I want to hug him, and that's a really bad idea.

"It meant a lot to me." His hand trails down my arm to my fingers.

Heat crawls up my face. I give his hand a quick squeeze and let go.

I invite Sophie and Tim, but they are my only friends at Calvin's party. I know his friends in passing, but it's not like I *know them* know them. Someone brings beer, and I carry one around like I'm drinking it, but I don't like the taste. Besides, I have to drive myself home later.

"Will you hate me if we bail?" Sophie asks.

"Yes," I say. "Don't leave me alone. There are only two other girls, and they've barely come up for air." They're making out with their boyfriends at opposite ends of the living room.

Cal and his two best friends, Joey and Drew, are playing pool in the bonus room. I'm sitting on a barstool watching. Tim has just finished off the last of his third piece of cake, and Sophie has been going through the playlist on Cal's phone because she hates the classic rock music that I chose to play, but there's not much else on there.

"Why do y'all like this stuff?" she asks. Her tastes lean more toward country.

Music is one of those things that Cal and I totally agree on. "How can you not?"

"Look. I came. I said, 'Happy Birthday.' I ate some cake. I'm done."

I sigh and make puppy dog eyes and poke out my bottom lip, but it does no good.

"I'm done. I don't know these people, and I'm bored."

"Fine. Leave me to suffer alone."

She turns her head to Tim, "She's discovered our master plan, right babe?"

Tim downs the rest of his beer then lowers his voice. "Date a jerk, suffer alone. That's just the way it works."

"Real nice, Tim. I hope that cake and beer combo makes you sick, you freeloader," I tease. I walk with them to the front door. "Seriously. Drive safe."

Sophie takes his keys from his pocket. "I'm safe." She hugs me. "Have fun," she says with a big cheesy smile.

"I hate you," I say.

"I love you, too," she says.

I should have known inviting them was a bad idea. Our double date to the drive-in in the summer was a disaster. We brought folding chairs and sat in front of Tim's truck. For a while it was fun. We ate dinner as we waited for the sun to set so the movie could start.

The drive-in speaker played a trivia game, and Calvin and Sophie got pretty competitive. She was better than him with the pop culture stuff, and the science questions were a toss-up. I went to get us some ice cream and got back just in time to stop Sophie's claws from coming out.

I could hear her voice from two cars away and could tell by her tone that Cal must have said something awful. "So here's a question you should know the answer to, how many *other people* did you see when you broke up with Madison last spring?"

"No one as worthy as Madison," Cal answered, his eyes on me. He stood and met me at the back of the truck, taking his ice cream cone.

"You mean no one who was willing to be a sugar mama for you?"

I gave her a sizzling glare. "Sophie. Stop it."

"No. I meant no one with any taste. But I'm sure you can't relate considering your taste runs redneck."

I couldn't believe he said that. "Calvin! That is so out of line. You need to apologize."

Tim stood, and Sophie stepped in front of him. "At least he has a job and doesn't make me pay."

There was a horribly long, thick silence. Tim was clenching and unclenching his fists, Sophie's face was stony, but Cal was actually grinning. Then he gave this snorty, sort of chuckle.

"I was just kidding around. Y'all are so uptight. Okay, fine." He inclined his head to Sophie. "I apologize." He held out the ice cream cone to her. "You take it. I'm willing to admit that you won the trivia game. Let it be the prize."

The speaker crackled, and a preview started on the screen. Someone shouted at us to sit down. Sophie looked at me, and I pleaded with my eyes for her to let it drop. She took the ice cream without a word. The rest of us followed her lead. By the end of the movie everyone seemed to be back to normal. Cal didn't even take the bait when they dropped us off at his car in the Pansy's parking lot and Sophie said, "Have fun, kids. Don't do anything I wouldn't do." But I think he was biting his tongue.

I should've learned my lesson. I guess I'm an optimist.

I decide to do some clean-up since Calvin and three of his friends have gone into his room to watch livestream gameplay—Cal's favorite pastime, and four others have taken over the pool table. I pick up the empties and other trash lying around, consolidate what's left of the food on the snack table, and take the empty punch bowl to the kitchen to wash.

When I'm finished, I go to Calvin's room, but stop short outside the partially open door when I hear, "Don't tell Madison, okay? She'll make a big deal out of it."

I don't have to look; the smell tells me that they're passing around a joint. I don't mind him drinking a little, but other drugs are way out of my comfort zone. He knows I don't do drugs. I know pot's not one of the scary drugs, but if too much drinking turns him mean, what will a combination of drugs do?

I hear Joey say, "Man, sometimes I wish we'd never gone to that frat party at Vandy this summer. You'd still be a free agent with tales of college tail to tell instead of being on a leash."

"Don't go there unless you want to talk about what the X did to you," Cal said.

My chest feels tight and it's hard to breathe, but I'm sure it has nothing to do with the putrid pot stench coming out of his room. *The party at Vandy? Where dance camp was? The X?*

I'm not sure I want to know.

He was so great, so sweet, before his friends arrived. I'm beginning to hate his friends as much as he hates mine. I leave without saying goodbye.

How long will it be before he even misses me?

Will he miss me?

I'm thankful to find that no one is blocking me in, they all parked in the grass. Cal's dad pulls in the driveway beside my car as I'm getting in. He's in a suit, but his tie is loosened. When I start my car, his eyes meet mine. I smile and wave, but he doesn't acknowledge it. He seems to be gathering his things. Maybe he's distracted. Maybe he can't see me as clearly as I can see him. He gets out carrying his suit jacket, a briefcase, and a beer bottle. He takes a long pull from the bottle and meets my eyes again with a glare. He lifts the bottle like he's toasting me. I smile again and wave, like it's totally fine that he can't even give me a smile. I guess getting a job didn't stop the drinking or change his personality back to the way it supposedly was before.

Relieved that I'm no longer in the house and won't have to deal with him, I drive away and don't look back.

I turn off my phone when I get home.

Chapter Seven

I don't hear from him until around noon on Saturday. I almost don't answer the call.

"How mad are you?" he asks, like he's trying to figure out what level of apology is required.

"Why do you think I'm mad?"

"You didn't even say goodbye. How do you think that made me look, when I couldn't find you, and my dad announced that you'd left?"

"I'm sorry. I guess I was a little upset."

"Why?"

"To be honest I was worried we were going to have a repeat of the end of the summer party at Joey's."

He sighs so loud I can practically hear his eyes roll. "I don't remember what happened at Joey's."

"I can't forget it." My mind flashes on the cold, smug look on his face that night, and I close my eyes. "O, call not me to justify the wrong, that thy unkindness lays upon my heart." I hear a little grumble from him about the quote.

"You sure know how to hold a grudge. I've apologized a hundred times for that. You know I would never hurt you on purpose. What else are you mad about? It can't just be that."

"Well, I heard you say that you didn't want me to know you were smoking pot because I would make a big deal out of it. So I'm wondering what else you've kept from me." *Like the Vandy party.*

He swears under his breath. "Nothing. Jeez. Way to make my point. I just took one hit. I couldn't let the guys think I was whipped." I don't say anything. "I thought you were mad because I wasn't paying attention to you."

"Leaving me alone with a bunch of your friends that completely ignored me wasn't exactly nice, but I get that you haven't seen everybody since Joey's party, and you miss them too. I wanted you to have fun."

"You had Sophie and her redneck."

"I've asked you not to call him that."

"I'm sorry, Mads, really. I blew it last night. I should have paid more attention to you. You planned the whole thing, bought all the food. It was amazing. You're amazing. I love you, baby. You mean everything to me."

How can I stay mad when he says stuff like that?

"Let me take you out as a thank you. We can go to the movies and dinner tonight. I'll pick you up at 3:30."

"I can't let you spend your birthday money on me."

"Okay then, we'll pick up subs and stream something. It doesn't matter as long as it's just the two of us. I've missed you like crazy. Now that I've had a chance to hang out with my friends, I'm all yours."

"I thought your mom wanted to spend the day with you."

"I'm going over there when we hang up."

"Then you better pick me up at 5:00, so she doesn't get upset."

"She won't. She loves you too."

He's trying extra hard to be sweet and lets me choose the movie and the sub for us to split. He opens doors for me, holds my hand. We go back to his house and settle down in his room to watch and eat. There's leftover cake too, which is always a good thing.

His parents went in together and got him a new laptop. It sits on his desk, still in the box. If it were mine, I'd have personalized it already. I know he's excited about it because it's faster than his old laptop and has a special keyboard, which means he can play those multi-player games online instead of just watching others play. Sounds better than watching, but apparently, watching is a huge, global hobby. He gets so involved watching that he forgets everything else. Even me. I worry playing the games will be worse.

After the movie, we're in the house alone and start kissing. I break all the rules I've made for myself and allow him to lead me to his bed. I know that it's stupid to put myself in such a tempting situation, but I've missed him so much, it's hard to listen to that voice in my head. At first, I protest when he tries to take off my shirt, but as things heat up, I give in.

We're so into each other we don't even hear his older sister Lyla drive up or come in the front door. We jerk apart when she knocks twice and opens his bedroom door.

"Hey little brother, I came by to wish—oh, sorry." She closes the door. "You really ought to lock this if you're going to be doing that," she says from the other side with a nervous laugh.

I scramble into my shirt, but it's too late. She has seen me half-naked, and I am mortified. I'm sure my face is bright red.

"I'll never be able to look her in the eyes again."

"It's no big deal. She's twenty-three. She'll understand."

But she doesn't. She calls us into the living room and decides to give us a lecture on the importance of being prepared with protection. I want to sink into the couch and drown. Cal thinks it's hysterical and bites his lip in an attempt not to smile the whole time.

"I want to go home," I say when she leaves us.

He stops smiling. "It's only eight thirty. And I have to leave in the morning."

"You can come stay at my house for a while, but I'm not staying here."

"You're overreacting. Like you always do. It's not a big deal."

I just give him a look and go to his room to get my purse. He follows me in and shuts and locks the door. "Now that we know all about practicing safe sex, let's do a little *more* practice." He pushes me onto the bed, lifts up my shirt and starts blowing on my belly, tickling me.

"No. I want to go home," I say between giggles. "I can't believe you locked the door."

He kisses my belly and looks up with this devilish smile. "She told me to."

"She's going to think we went right back to it."

"Let's not disappoint her." He positions himself over me and starts kissing me, but I turn my head. He doesn't give up that easily. He focuses on my neck.

I push him away. "I want to go home, Cal. Please? I could really use your help with my calculus homework anyway."

He lets himself fall to the bed with a sigh. "Fine. I'll take you home, but only if you pay for my tutoring services with a little…" His hand slips under my shirt, and he kisses me again until we're both all hot.

"I think we can come to an arrangement." He starts to pull off my shirt, but I stop him. "Not here."

He groans. "Let's go then."

After I locate my purse and shoes and we're headed to his car, something occurs to me. "I bet you could make a little money tutoring people at school."

He frowns, and I'm afraid that I've touched a nerve, but then he gives me a slick smirk. "Or they could pay me with other things."

I shove him playfully. "They better not."

He opens the car door for me. "You would have me turn away poor, helpless girls failing their classes?"

He lets me think about that while he walks around to the driver's side and gets in. And I can't help but picture the half-naked girls he told me about that walk around his co-ed dorm, inviting him into their rooms. "Never mind. Forget I mentioned it."

But it gets me thinking. He was a party boy in high school. And he did break up with me to see other people.

"Cal?"

He reaches over and takes my hand. "Hmm?"

"How many girls have you…been with?"

"It doesn't matter. They didn't mean anything to me. They were just drunken one-night stands." He brings my hand to his lips. "I've only ever loved *you*."

That doesn't make me feel better. "How many?"

"Mads, come on. You don't really want to know."

Now I'm imagining the worst. "Just tell me."

"Four or five. Okay?"

No, it's not okay. He doesn't even know for sure? It's not a beautiful, sacred gift to him. It's just a short-term pleasure. My chest feels tight and heavy. Tears sting the corners of my eyes.

It's not that I think I'm going to hell if I have sex with Cal, but I do think it's a sin. I don't want to purposefully sin. I do enough sinning by accident. And I believe sex is a seal of the marriage covenant and doing it with anyone besides your husband is adultery. Even if you're not married yet, it's still sex *outside* of marriage. I want to be faithful to my husband and to God.

"See. Now you're mad."

"No, I—did you even care about any of them?"

"No. You were my first girlfriend. I didn't even realize I cared about you until after I'd lost you."

"You didn't lose me. You broke up with me."

"Dang Madison, you're very intense. I wasn't ready for a serious relationship then. You freaked me out."

"You don't think having sex with someone qualifies as a serious relationship?"

"No. Not if it's just a hook-up, and both of you know that going in."

"But you're ready for a serious relationship now?"

"You know I am. Wow. How can you even ask me that?"

"I'm sorry. It's just…you're four hours away and you just told me that sex doesn't equal serious to you. You could be up there having drunken hook-ups for all I know."

He starts laughing. "You're a piece of work." He squeezes my hand. "You're four hours away from me too, you know."

"Touché."

Chapter Eight

At dance team practice, I'm feeling my added workout time at home. Every move is torture for the first ten minutes or so until I'm fully warmed up. As dance team captain I'm in charge, and even though I don't want to stop moving, I give them a quick water break before going through our routines. I keep dancing, though.

"Take a break, Madison, you're making the rest of us look bad," Chloe says. She's the dark-haired, dark-eyed Latina Barbie to all-star Ken Reynolds, the homeroom hottie. Some people even call her Barbie behind her back. No one would dare say it to her face.

I grab my water bottle and go to the circle of eight girls on the floor at the back of the room and slide into the splits beside Chloe to continue stretching and moving. "I'm too sore. I don't want to get stiff." I take a few gulps of water.

Ken Reynolds stops in the doorway and holds up his phone and then points back and forth between himself and Chloe. She narrows her eyes and shoots him a bird. Several of the girls laugh. Ken's face falls, and he stomps away.

"Did you guys break up?" I ask her.

"Not yet. But I think he cheated on me. I just don't have any proof."

I'm not sure what to say. "I'm sorry."

"He's the one that's sorry. He swears he didn't do it." She lies back on the floor. "Maybe I'm overreacting."

I push a few stray hairs that have come loose back into my pony-tail holder and just wait to see if she wants to tell me anything else. I mean, it's not like we're close friends.

"Everyone says I'd be crazy to break up with him," she says.

I nod, smiling. "He *is* Ken Reynolds. But hey, you're Chloe

Salazar. You shouldn't have to put up with any crap. And cheating's non-negotiable. Besides, you could have any guy you want."

She grins and sits up, lightly shoving my shoulder. "That's what I'm talking about."

"What makes you think he cheated?" I lay the side of my face on the cool wood floor and stretch my arms toward my toes.

"I just found out that Lisa Purdue has a lake house down the road from his, and they were both there Labor Day weekend." She leans back against the bench and pulls her legs into the butterfly position. "I wouldn't care, except yesterday at lunch, I saw her give him a look. Like a *we're sharing a secret* kind of look. And you know how she is."

I sit up and shrug. "I know how people say she is."

"Well, it's true. She doesn't have any problem sleeping with someone else's boyfriend. I know lots of relationships she's ruined."

"But Ken says he didn't, right?" I see Ken every morning, and we occasionally share a few flirty words, but we don't have actual conversations. Would those silly flirtations look like something more to Chloe? "Do you trust him?"

Ms. Vaughan claps her hands, our signal to get up. Chloe sighs as she pulls herself to her feet. "I want to."

Trust is the thing. Having been untrustworthy myself once, I'm super cautious about giving my trust to people. But you have to trust the people you love. You have to. So I guess I have to trust Calvin to make good use of his time. I shouldn't worry that he's watching and playing games online all day. And I should believe him when he says he doesn't have time to call me much because of schoolwork. *And I guess I have to trust that he's not having drunken hook-ups in his dorm full of half-naked girls.*

After practice, Ms. Vaughan comes back from wherever she goes during practice. She's not much of a dancer but was the only one willing to sponsor us. I do most of the choreography, unless she uses the stuff she's taught at coach camp. Chloe's a good choreographer too, adding in lots of tumbling moves that I don't know much about. I wonder what Ms. Vaughan will do next year when we're gone.

"Seniors," she says, "be sure and look for audition information posted about dance teams at the colleges you've applied to if you want to be on them. The details may not be up yet, but keep an eye on it. Most tryouts for the following school year are in the spring. You may even have to spend the weekend there."

Great. Another thing to worry about. Another choice that has to be made. If I'm going to UT with Cal, I'll definitely want to be on the dance team—it's the only dance they have. They don't even a dance minor. But auditions for Company Two aren't until May. And what if I don't make it the first time I try out? That will cause a whole host of other problems.

Should I go ahead and apply to UT as a back-up? I wish I had someone to talk to about it. I should be able to talk to Cal, but I'm still not ready to drop that bomb on him. And Sophie is as practical as my parents. I feel like I need a concrete plan, not a hopeful dream before I tell her. Besides, I barely see her now that marching band competition season has started.

I go by the counselor's office, but she's gone for the day. I'll have to catch her another time. I really need some answers to all these questions in my head.

I've been spending a lot of my spare time with Kayleigh and Kaitlyn. She and Derrick still haven't resolved their argument, but they've started counseling with their pastor. She wants to become a midwife which requires finishing nursing school then getting her master's in nurse-midwifery. Derrick doesn't believe there are enough people out there that even want to do that for all that schooling to be worth it.

It's the first Saturday in October, and surprisingly, it's not too hot. Fall may actually have come to stay. We take Kaitlyn to the Greenway. Multiple paths run along the river and wind around our town for miles. This one has a playground where we plan to stop for a while.

Kayleigh walks quickly on the paved path, pushing the stroller in front of her. "I don't have much left of nursing school, which I only dropped out of because I got pregnant and was so sick. He knows this." She walks even faster, and her grip on the stroller gets tighter. "Does he think because I'm a mother now I don't want to do anything else with my life?"

"Would you have to stop working entirely to finish school? Maybe he just wants you to wait until Kaitlyn's older and in school, so childcare won't cost so much."

"Yeah. It would be a stretch for a little while. I get that. But now is the best time because we want to have more kids. It'll just be harder and more complicated later."

She parks the stroller in front of the dog park and faces me.

"Why do you think he's so against it all of a sudden?" I ask.

She looks pained. "I think he was always against my going to nursing school. I just didn't realize. Maybe he thought I'd forget about it once I had Kaitlyn. But I don't understand why. Is he threatened by my wanting more education? Or jealous because he didn't get to finish college either? But if I'm making good money, then he can go back to school if he wants to.

"Surely, he doesn't think we should wait until we're debt free. Because then it'll never happen. And Mom's willing to keep Kaitlyn while I'm training as long as my classes are after her school hours."

She sighs and squats down next to the stroller, putting on a fake smile. "See the doggies. What's a doggie say? *Ruff. Ruff.*" Kaitlyn claps her little hands and tries to imitate the sound.

I don't have any answers for Kayleigh. I think she just needs to vent. Maybe a change of subject will help her, and she might be the one with some answers for me. We start walking again. "Next weekend, I'm auditioning for *The Nutcracker.*"

"Which part?"

"All the good small parts are already taken by the City Ballet students, and all the hard parts are taken by their company, so you audition just to be in it. Then they make you a party goer or a mouse or they put you in one of the international dances." I shrug. "I'm happy to do whatever. I just want to get to know some of the teachers and choreographers better."

Her face crinkles with confusion. "How come?"

"You promise not to tell Mom and Dad?"

A bicycle rider comes by, and we move to the side.

"Okay?" she says like she's not sure.

I pick a flower from a vine hanging from a tree. *Quit stalling.* "I want to try out for their company in May."

Her eyes get big, and her eyebrows shoot up. "What about teaching?"

"I want to dance, Kayleigh. Professionally." There I said it. It's out there. She doesn't respond, but I can tell she's trying to decide what to say as we start walking again. "The problem is that I'm not good enough—yet. I think I could be if I start in January with daily classes. But that would mean I'd have to quit dance team during basketball season. And it's expensive."

"You need to talk to Mom and Dad about this. Especially Mom. She's going to flip out."

"I know." I don't even want to think about her reaction. "I was hoping to get some positive feedback from *The Nutcracker* chore-ographer first."

"That's a good idea. But you need to at least put some hints out there now. Dad's always been very supportive of your dancing. Maybe you could start with him."

"Yeah. Maybe. I did bring up classes to Mom. She said it was a waste of money." I kick a rock off the path into the grass. "Dad usually caves to what Mom wants."

She nods thoughtfully. "True. But if it's what you're passionate about, you should go for it. What's Calvin think?"

I sigh. "I don't think he'll like it. He's looking forward to my coming to UT."

She looks at me sideways. "You haven't told him either?"

I put my arm around her. "You're the lucky first recipient of the news. Aren't you special?" I give her a big cheesy grin.

She puts on a thick southern drawl and puts a hand to her heart. "Why, I am so honored to be your guinea pig, darlin'."

We both laugh, which makes Kaitlyn giggle, which makes us laugh harder. "But seriously, Maddy, you should tell him. If he's going to be a part of your future, you need to be on the same page about your plans." She narrows her eyes at me. "What's going on with this guy, anyway? You don't seem very certain about this relationship. Is he even a Christian?"

I sigh. Should've known she'd ask that. "Not yet. Don't you think my influence could lead him to the Lord, though?"

"Oh, Maddy. The Bible says that a believer shouldn't marry a non-believer. That's because God wants the best for us. Marriage is hard enough already, why make it harder? I know I've been ranting today, and I appreciate you listening, but nothing is more important to me than my marriage. That talk we had with Mom and Dad helped us re-focus on our commitment to each other. We're praying about it. Talking to our pastor. We will work it out. But it's only because of our faith that we can put aside our own selfish desires and find a compromise." She's quiet for a few minutes then asks, "Is that why you're not sure if you're in love with him? Because he's not a believer?"

"That's part of it. I think we're just having a hard time right now because of the separation. It's hard to be on the same page when you hardly ever see each other. I just don't know if our relationship can survive my following my dream."

"Then maybe it's not strong enough to survive marriage either."

Cal's gone from texting me all the time to barely responding to my texts, and his calls get shorter and shorter. I asked him not to call after 10:00. At first, he was calling every night around 9:00, but now, it's more like ten minutes before 10:00, if not right at 10:00 or a little after. Sometimes he doesn't call at all.

Yesterday, he complained that his roommate and his girlfriend were constantly in their room—in bed! He said he had to hang out in the library a lot to give them privacy. He wished it was next year, and I was there, so it could be us. *Seriously?* He also said that their having sex all the time makes him want me even more.

How am I supposed to respond to *that*?

And what does that say about Cal's feelings for me? Is that the only reason he wants to go out with me? Am I just a challenge to him?

Stop it, Maddy.

He loves me. I know he does. I can see it in his eyes. I can hear it in his voice. And I love him. He makes my stomach do a flip-flop when I see him. Lots of people make long-distance relationships work. If I make it into the company, we'd still have summers together.

Maybe I *can* have the dream and the guy.

Chapter Nine

$\mathcal{I}$m eating lunch with Nathan at work on Wednesday, and he asks what my plans are for the long weekend. We get Thursday and Friday off school for Fall break.

"Well, I'm working here, as usual, most of the time, but I'm auditioning for City Ballet's *Nutcracker* production Saturday. How about you?"

He takes a bite of his pizza and holds up a finger while he chews. "Wow. Which part?"

"I don't know." I explain about the good parts being taken already. "So I'll just have some tiny group part if I get to be in it."

"You will. You're a great dancer."

I dip my sub sandwich into the secret sauce and frown. "And you know this because…?"

"My sister took classes at Miss Gena's. I was forced to attend her recitals every year."

I feel the blush rise in my face. "Oh." I can't believe he's seen all of my recitals for the past three years. Even my parents only came for my solos and then left. His parents must be more like Sophie's. They drag her brother to everything she does, too. Poor Nathan. "Hope it wasn't too torturous. Did they let you bring a book or something?"

"Are you kidding? The little kids are hysterical. And the older dancers are good, except for some of the beginner classes." He makes a face. "Those were pretty lame."

"Did your sister find a new place to take classes?"

"She's playing the violin now. Talk about torture…" He puts his hands over his ears and gives me a pained expression. We both laugh. "You should open a studio to take Miss Gena's place. You taught a lot of classes for her, didn't you?"

I smile just thinking about it. The kids in their little tutus, choreographing, and choosing just the right music… "I did. I loved it too. I miss it a lot. I want to teach again someday."

He grins. "After you go to New York and dance on Broadway?"

I'm not sure if he's teasing or not. "No. But I would like to be in a professional company, hopefully City Ballet. I just…my parents won't go for it."

He wipes his hands and mouth and takes a final swallow of soda. "College isn't for everyone. My older brother's wife runs a day care center, and she just took some online business classes. If you can make a living doing what you love, that's the best anyone can hope for. That's what my dad always tells me. I'm going to study Wildlife Management with a minor in Recreation and be a park ranger or a guide or a game warden. Something outside. If I had to sit behind a desk all day, I'd lose my mind."

He gathers his trash as he stands. "You've got to make your parents understand that doing what makes you happy is the important thing. Not getting a useless degree in something you don't care about. God gives us passions and talents for a reason." He looks at my half-eaten sub. "You better hurry up."

He starts to walk away. "Nathan?" He turns back and raises his eyebrows. "Thanks." He just smiles.

How was that so easy? Because I'd already told my sister? Maybe it will get easier with every person I tell. My stomach twists at the thought.

Or not.

It was probably because his opinion doesn't matter. I should go around telling random strangers until I get used to saying it. Then it'll be easy to talk to my parents. I hope.

But I'm not sure it will ever be easy to tell Cal.

As I finish my lunch, I realize this is the same booth where Calvin and I met. He saw me here on my break singing to the old Journey song on the piped-in music.

"Not everyone appreciates Journey anymore," he said. "Do you just know the words because you hear it in here all the time or are you a fan?"

"My dad's a big fan. He plays a lot of '80s music at home. So I'm sort of a fan by association."

He sat across from me in the booth, and we talked about music for a while. It was nice. He was intelligent, not crude, and made me laugh. Not gorgeous, but he had those great eyes that contrasted with his black hair, and he was tall. I gave him my number, and the rest is history.

It was easy to talk to him. I could have told him then. Now it seems like a deal breaker, and I'm not ready to give up on our happily ever after if there is a way to have him *and* be a dancer. There's got to be a way.

Or maybe I'll get that sign. *Please let me have a sign.*

The auditions are at the City Ballet studio. We don't have to perform solos or anything. The teachers just observe as we do barre exercises and steps across the floor. Then one of the instructors demonstrates a combination for us to learn. Two teachers walk around—one of them is Ms. Turpin, who taught the Intensive this summer. They hold clipboards observing and making notes. I'm one of the oldest there and definitely the tallest, which makes me stand out, but I don't know whether that's good or bad.

Those of us that can, switch to pointe shoes for the next hour. There are only five of us left. The others were told whether or not they were in and when to be back for rehearsals. The teachers whisper a lot while we're dancing, and I get the feeling it's about me. One of them leaves the room for a little while and then comes back and nods. Ms. Turpin calls me over as the others change back to their street shoes and cover ups.

"You have very nice lines," she says. "I remember you from the Intensive."

"Thank you." My heart is in my throat, and my pulse is racing. I believe she's trying to let me down easy, and I'm blinking back the extra water forming in my eyes.

"Our problem is your height. You'll stick out if we put you with the other little ones. And our older, advanced students who are closer to your size have been practicing their group dances for a while already. Fortunately, we have another tall girl in our Intermediate class that the choreographer decided to add a place for as a parlor maid at the party. He was wishing that he had two so he could have one in each cast, though. He didn't want Tanya to have to be in every performance. She's only fifteen. We just called him and told him about you, and he was thrilled."

I swallow hard. He was thrilled about me? "You're giving me a special part? Is it *en pointe*?"

She smiles and nods. "It's a very small part in just one dance. Even though it's technically a solo part, there are a lot of other things going on at the same time, so it's not a solo performance. The others will be party guests or mice at the opening party and in the Russian dance or the Chinese dance. So they get to be in two, but they'll be in flats and in costumes that will make them impossible to pick out." She put her hands out like they are scales. "It evens out."

It sure does!

I float all the way home.

Mom takes one look at my face when I come into the kitchen and gives me a big hug.

"Congratulations. I made chocolate cake to celebrate."

"That was optimistic."

"There was never any doubt. You're a wonderful dancer." She eyes the cake with a frown. "It's a little lopsided. Maybe I should toss it and start over."

Really? "It's just for us, Mom. It doesn't matter what it looks like. It's chocolate."

"I guess." She gets out the spatula for icing it.

I tell her about the special part. And then I suck up my fears and say, "Mom, do you think I'm good enough to be in City Ballet?"

She frowns a little, but I don't know if it's because of my question or the icing that—heaven forbid—just plopped on the counter. "I don't think you could do that and go to college at the same time. Certainly not in Knoxville. And it would be hard to keep up with your training to do it after college. Impossible, really.

They require so many projects in Early Childhood Education. Maybe you can be on the dance team at UT. That would be fun." She hands me a spoon with some icing on it and smiles like the matter is settled.

I want to say that I meant be in the company *instead* of being a teacher.

But chicken out.

I take the spoon and lick the icing like a lollipop, but it's hard to get it past those words stuck in my throat.

After dinner, I push myself harder than ever at the barre. It was the perfect opportunity to tell her what I really wanted, and I blew it. *Stupid. Stupid. Stupid.* My foot slides in and out of fifth position with each word. *Coward. Coward. Coward.*

I tell Cal about the special part that night when he calls. And about rehearsals starting Monday. I'll go Monday, Tuesday, and Friday to the studio from 5:30-8:00 for the scene rehearsals and Saturdays from 1:00-5:00 for full cast rehearsal at the Tennessee Performing Arts Center.

"You'll be a beautiful parlor maid. You'll probably outshine Clara and get reviews written about you saying, "Why did they put the best dancer in the show in such a small part?"

"Sure they will." But I can't help the giggle that bubbles up in me. Then my bubble bursts because he has plans to go meet someone and go to a party, so he says goodbye. I'm glad he's made some friends, but I'd hoped since he called at 9:30 we'd have thirty minutes, not five.

I wait until Sunday after church to call Sophie since she was at a band competition Saturday night. When I do, she says, "You've got to get me comp tickets."

I roll my eyes even though she can't see. "I can't get comp tickets. It's just a tiny part. But they said family and friends could come to the full-dress rehearsal free. It's on a Tuesday night, though."

"I'll be there." I hear her mumble something to someone else. "You want to come to the movies with me and Tim?"

"I have to work. Five to close." I wonder if Nathan will be there and then remind myself that it doesn't matter. Just because he and I both deserve Academy Awards for the friendship we're pretending to have, doesn't mean I should believe in it.

"It stinks that we never see each other anymore," Sophie says. "And don't say, 'Just every day at school.' Because it's not the same. Dr. Northcutt may be oblivious to our note passing, but I want to hang out with you."

"I know. Maybe next Saturday night? After rehearsal?"

She says something else to Tim that I can't hear. "It's a date. Just you and me. Let's have a scary movie marathon in honor of Halloween."

"Sounds perfect!"

I have to finish my homework before I go to work, so we hang up. But the warm and fuzzy feeling about the special part stays with me all afternoon. Later, when I get to work, Nathan starts to give me a hug but switches to a high five when I tell him. We laugh and my face gets hot. So awkward.

Since I had to close at work, I call Cal on my drive home, but he doesn't answer. He didn't text me all day either. *Where is he? What's he doing? Asleep? Another party? Still hungover from yesterday's party?* I try to sleep but toss and turn for about an hour and then poetry comes into my head. I used to write poetry all the time, but it hasn't come to me like this since—Nathan. I know I won't be able to rest until I scribble down the verse.

> *Fenced in my shame*
>> *I don't look to the greener grass*
> *Anymore.*
>> *This grass is nice too.*
> *It cushions my falls*
>> *Each time I catch a glimpse*
> *By accident*
>> *And slip on what might have been.*

I tear the paper out of the notebook and shove it in the shoebox under my bed. It's already brimming with other poems. I've stopped trying to figure out what they mean, but I can't bring myself to throw them away. They are pieces of me.

Chapter Ten

$\mathscr{I}$t's our first rehearsal in the theatre. I love the theatre so much. Even without the sets, it lights my whole heart on fire: the expanse of the stage, the view of all those seats. And the wings. I love the wings.

The girl that plays Clara is named Megan, and she's really good. I remember her from the Summer Intensive. We're the same age, but she lives in Nashville and has been taking classes with City Ballet for years. I loved Miss Gena, but she wasn't as strict as the teachers at the Intensive.

We're rehearsing with piano music only instead of the orchestra we'll have for the actual show. I hear my cue, and my imagination takes over. I bourrée out with my feather duster in hand. I'm the only one on stage to start, and all eyes are on me for about twenty seconds. Attitude and arch, soutenu turn, sissonne, arabesque. Then, several men from the company enter as butlers bringing the huge Christmas tree and other decorations. One hands me a wreath. I pas-de-chat back and forth, peeking around the wreath before I hang it on a fireplace at the back.

Clara and her family enter and dance around, pointing and exclaiming over the decorations and their own festive clothes, while I hang stockings in the background. Then, they are supposed to line up to prepare to greet guests, and I'm supposed to go and pretend to open a door for the guests arriving, but the family is in the way. We haven't practiced together before.

The music stops. The spell is broken. We're all in boring leotards. The only real prop I have is the feather duster. The tree is an empty platform on wheels. The wreath, a hoop. The fireplace is there. The same one they've used for ten years. It needs re-painting.

Brett Donelly, the choreographer, is probably in his fifties, with salt and pepper hair, but his body looks like that of a thirty-year-old. Perfectly toned. "Okay," he says in his gravelly smoker's voice. "That looked pretty good for our first run together. Madison, start on the other side of the fireplace to hang the stockings then come stage left to get around them. Don't forget there will be furniture wherever there is blue tape on the floor. I think you turned right into the couch."

"Oh, yeah. Sorry." I steal a glance at Megan. She's smirking. I gulp and look at my feet.

"It's fine. Next Saturday we'll have more props." He starts telling Megan and the others all the things they did wrong, too. I don't feel so bad after that.

That's the only scene I'm in, but I stay after they move on to the next scene because I love watching it come together. Ms. Turpin asks if I'll run to the studio for her. She forgot her roll book for the show and needs to make sure all the little ones are accounted for, during and after rehearsal.

I have to drive, but it's only a mile or so away. The traffic is awful because it's Saturday. I hate driving in downtown Nashville. People are everywhere. So much construction and so many one-way streets. It's a nightmare.

She gave me her keys, which makes me feel like I'm the studio owner as I climb the stairs to the back entrance. In her office, I grab the roll book. Under it, there's a desk calendar with the November page, but you can see the first week of December. She has a note in the December 7th box that reads: *Scholarship Auditions.*

I rush back to the theatre, and after I check off that all the kids are there, I find Ms. Turpin talking to the pianist and wait nearby, my heart racing. Finally, she walks away, and I run to her side.

"Ms. Turpin?"

"Thank you, Madison." She takes the roll book from me. "Everyone here?"

"Yes. Um, do you offer scholarships for classes?"

"We do," she says. "Every semester. Only one scholarship per person and only for one semester."

That's all I need. "And when are the auditions for classes starting this January?" I hold my breath.

"Because *Nutcracker* rehearsals are on Saturday, I have to do them on a Sunday, December seventh. Are you interested?"

"Yes, ma'am."

"It'll be at the studio at three o'clock. I'll put you down."

"Thank you."

She walks on, and I chassé the other way, feeling like I could float. Mom can't say no if the classes are free, right? I am so psyched when I leave.

I'm all gross from rehearsal, but I have to pick up the pizza for my night with Sophie. I already called ahead. I dash inside with my wallet and keys to find Nathan working the register.

"You don't look like a counter girl," I say with a grin.

He bats his eyes. "How about now?"

I laugh and look around. "Where is everyone? It's Saturday night. You're about to be slammed." I was able to leave rehearsal a little early so it's only 5:00, but shift change is at 4:30.

"Sandy called in sick, and Laurie is in the office taking off her nail polish. Scott broke his ankle this morning skateboarding." He gets my pizza and rings me up. "Abdulla's been calling people. Maybe you could work?"

"No way. Sophie and I are having some much-needed BFF time: pizza and a horror movie marathon." I tap my debit card and punch in my PIN.

He makes a face. "How can you watch those things? If I want blood and gore, I'd rather see realistic war movie classics like *Braveheart* or *Saving Private Ryan*."

"Ugh. I can't watch those because they're too real. Old horror movies are stupid, but suspenseful. And the gore is pretty fake in the old ones. I'm talking *Friday the 13th* and *Halloween*. That's just good scary fun."

"You're seriously screwed up." He hands the pizza to me. "Enjoy your pizza and have a nice evening." He says it with a fake feminine voice as he bats his eyes again.

"Uh, look who's talking." We both stop laughing abruptly when

Abdulla comes walking over. I hold the pizza up. "Can't work. I've got plans," I tell him.

He takes in my leotard and sweats, my hair in a messy bun, and my lack of makeup. "Hot date?" He snickers, but I'm already to the door.

"Ha, ha! See you Monday." I duck out.

After Sophie and I scream and flinch through *Halloween*, we decide to watch a chick flick we've both been wanting to see. It turns out to be pretty lame, though, so we turn it off and go in my room to talk. We lay next to each other facing opposite directions across my queen-sized bed.

"I want to tell you something, but I want you to hear me out first," Sophie says.

"Sounds serious. Are you breaking up with me?" I joke.

She makes a face. "Sort of. Maybe breaking a promise." She won't look at me. "I think Tim and I are going to…take the next step."

I know she's talking about sex, and my heart sinks. How am I supposed to stay strong if she's giving in? We promised we would help each other stand strong and not cave to our hormones, so I don't know what I'm supposed to say. "Are you asking me to talk you out of it?"

"No. I've been thinking about it, and I still think the Bible is clear that we aren't supposed to have sex *outside* of marriage. But what if you want to marry the person? What if you know you're going to marry the person. Tim is the one. I know he is. I can't imagine my future without him. So, maybe that's a workaround. Maybe it's not a sin if you marry the one you have sex with before marriage."

She grabs my pillows and bunches them up behind her head and finally looks at me.

"I thought you wanted to wait until after you graduate and become a vet before getting married. That's a long time from now. What if you change your mind about him by then?"

"I won't. And maybe we can get married before then. We're going to the same school. We both know what we want to do. We could live in married housing."

"Why are you so sure?" I'm not sure of anything when it comes to Cal.

"I don't really know how to describe it. We just fit. I feel it in my bones. I never want to be with anyone but him." She grins. "We finish each other's sandwiches."

I laugh at the *Frozen* reference. Do Cal and I have that kind of connection? I'll have to think about that later. "I promised to talk you out of it."

She sighs. "I know. I release you from the promise. I just don't understand how it could be a sin when I love him so much."

"The argument for that is: it *is* a sin, whether it *feels* like it or not, and if you love him so much, you'll still love him in three or four years, so there's no reason to have sex now. You have the rest of your lives—after you get married—to have sex."

"I know. But there's no *reason* to wait if I'm sure, right? Waiting is hard. No one else even cares. Is God really going to count sex inside a love relationship as sin? Maybe He's just talking about adultery and hook-ups. Did you hear Kylie and Tucker are getting married before the baby comes? They did things out of order, but it still worked out."

"See. Babies! Another reason not to have sex before marriage."

"Yeah," she says. "That would spin my life in a different direction. Maybe I need to think about it some more."

I don't want to let her off the hook so easily. I promised I wouldn't. But I know her well enough to know it takes a lot to change her mind. Maybe reverse psychology? "So, if I decide to marry Cal, you'd be okay with me taking the next step too? Because I could definitely see us married, living in college housing while he's in med school. It would be awesome."

"Oh, Maddy, no. You can't marry *him*. He is not the one." She shakes her head. "I won't go there." She mashes her lips together and squeezes her eyes tight. Then she starts kicking her feet like she's going to bust if she doesn't say what's on her mind. "I have to go there." She sits up and pulls me up too, resting her arms on my shoulders. "I'm only saying this because you are my best friend, and I love you. He's an arrogant, selfish, spoiled little former rich boy who floated through life without any problems until his parents got divorced and cut him off. Now you're paying his way, and it's like he expects it. Because he's always gotten what he wants when he wants it. He's never had to work for anything."

She leans in closer. "I thought college might make him grow up. Maybe it will. Maybe there's still hope. But would you at least consider the possibility that if you end up with him, you are going to be taking care of him, supporting him, putting yourself last for the rest of your life? And not the other way around. And I guarantee that will get old."

I pull away. *Wow.* That didn't go like I thought. I guess I never realized how much she truly hates Cal. "Only if he goes to med school. I mean, I might have to put him through school, but then he'll make lots of money as a doctor, and I won't have to work anymore. I could teach dance and have kids." I wouldn't be able to be in a dance company, though. Dance company members don't make enough to put someone through med school. They barely make enough to survive. "You don't know him like I do."

"I know you, though. And you are not yourself around him. I don't know who you are. I feel like you're trying too hard to make it work. I get that he's got the whole smoldering eyes thing going on—it's hot. But I don't see anything beyond the physical that makes you compatible. And you can't base a marriage on just that."

"How can you say that? We like the same music, the same movies, the same books. We never run out of things to talk about. We hardly ever argue. He's so sweet to me. I'm committed to making this work, that's all. You've never seen me try because this is the first time since Nathan that I've loved someone." I had already told her about my humiliating experience in front of his sister. "The other night he took me home when I asked. He didn't push. He didn't even get mad."

She falls back to the pillows. "Because he didn't have any right to be mad—you did. And he wasn't sweet at that end of the summer party. He's so condescending too. That's not sweet. It's disrespectful. And you just forgive and forget like it's nothing."

"True love forgives. It wasn't his fault his sister walked in on us.

Why should I be mad about that? And he was drunk at Joey's party, so he acted out of character." I'm glad I didn't tell her the whole truth about that incident.

"I'm not sure he has any character. He's such a jerk. And forgiveness doesn't mean being a doormat. Why did he put you in a compromising situation in the first place? Why didn't he stand up for you against his sister? Huh? Why didn't he tell her to mind her own business instead of letting her embarrass you further? She had no right to lecture you. I would have gone off on the girl."

I shrug. "She was just being a big sister." Sophie is the big sister. She doesn't understand that big sisters are super protective.

She throws her arm over her eyes and sighs. "Whatever. Guys should protect their girlfriends, defend them, always look out for them. Does Cal ever take care of you? Like last night, Tim was with my parents at the game, and I ran over to say hi. My mom immediately started ragging on me because I dropped my flag during the show. And Tim was like, 'She slipped in that mud puddle. I don't know how she didn't fall. Dropping her flag was hardly a big deal. She could've twisted her ankle. Are you okay?' And he put his arm around me and looked at her like she was being mean, which she was." She giggles. "You should have seen her face."

"I think it's part of a wife's responsibility to take care of her husband. My mom takes care of my dad. And look how happy they are."

"Hello? You're not married to the boy yet. When people are dating, they're on their best behavior. Is this his best? That's a scary thought. Besides it's reciprocal. Your dad takes care of your mom too, right? Your parents are happy and a real example of true love. Can't you see that isn't what you have with Cal? When does Cal ever treat you like your dad treats your mom? Like you're special?" I frown as I think about that. He makes me feel special every time he tells me he loves me and every time he makes me feel desirable.

She shakes her head at me. "You're so oblivious. I guess love *is* blind."

I put the back of my hand dramatically across my forehead. "O me, what eyes hath Love put in my head, which have no correspondence with true sight."

"I'm on the same page with William? Who'da thunk it?" She checks the time on her phone. "I think we need ice cream. Death by chocolate, preferably." She scoots to the end of my bed. "Come on. Baskin-Robbins doesn't close for twenty minutes."

We slip on our flip-flops and run for the car.

I don't sleep much. Between Sophie kicking me—she's all over the bed when she sleeps—and what she said to me earlier, it just isn't happening. I keep thinking about what my sister said about marrying a man who supports your dreams and not marrying a non-believer. Then Sophie saying that I deserve a man who will defend me and take care of me, treat me as if I'm special.

I don't know if Calvin would support my dreams because I'm too chicken to find out. I hope my steady faith is going to help influence him to seek God. I've been praying God would show him who He is. I *think* he would defend me and take care of me now, but I *know* he would if he was a Christian. What if we break up over that and he becomes a Christian next year? Or we break up over his not supporting my dreams, and then I'm not good enough to be in the company anyway? I sure could use a crystal ball.

Or a sign.

God, please give me a sign.

Chapter Eleven

*T*he next weekend, Calvin hitches a ride home with a friend. I don't get to see him Saturday because of rehearsal, and then I have to work. He's supposed to stop by and see me before we close. Joey's at the Pansy waiting for him. I guess they have plans.

I *screw my courage to the sticking place*, as Shakespeare would say, and come up behind Joey at the pinball machine in the back.

"Can I ask you something?"

He knocks the machine with his hip and swears as the ball rolls away. "Sure. What's the problem?"

I rub the pinball machine with my dish cloth like I'm cleaning it, so I don't have to look at him. "I overheard you say something about a frat party at Vandy."

He laughs. "Yeah? What about it? You gonna give the boy grief about stuff that happened when he wasn't with you?"

"You made it sound like it had something to do with Cal and me getting back together."

"That it did."

"How?"

"Why don't you ask him?"

Because I'm not sure he'll tell me the truth.

I give him my best *don't mess with me* glare. "I'm asking you."

"Fine. The party was on Saturday night, but we didn't go home until Monday, and we aren't too clear on all that happened in-between." He lowers his voice. "Sunday, we tried some Molly. Kind of like a hair-of-the-dog thing cuz we were hung-over."

"What's that?"

"Pure Ecstasy, baby." I'm still frowning. "X. MDMA. It makes you all touchy-feely, emotional, and crap. At some point, Cal saw that you were there Sunday. I guess y'all were checking into your camp or something, and he got all nostalgic for you, so he made me stay another night, so he could come to your practice Monday and see if you might be willing to hook up with him again."

So the grand gesture that I thought he made by coming to camp was not so grand.

"You look ticked. You're not gonna—"

"No. It's fine. I'm not mad. Thanks for telling me." I rush back to the kitchen. I'm really not mad. I'm disappointed. He didn't seek me out. He happened to see me when he was in a drug-induced emotional state, and he decided he wanted me back. Was it real? Was anything he said to me that day that convinced me to get back with him really what he felt? Maybe he doesn't love me. Maybe he's just using me because I'm willing to pay for everything like Sophie thinks.

Well, I'm not paying for anything now. I've got to save for classes. Who knows if I'll get the scholarship?

I don't see Joey leave, but Cal comes in about thirty minutes before closing time. He waves to me and points to the parking lot. I get Abdulla to let me go outside to see him for five minutes if I promise to polish the brass railings along with all my regular closing duties.

I just need to see in his eyes that he loves me.

"Hey, baby," he says, when I run over to him. He's leaning against one of his friends' cars, and they're all standing around talking. "They spring you early?"

"No, I just begged for a five-minute break, so I could come see you."

He pulls me up against him and kisses me passionately. He tastes like beer. His hands move down to my butt and press my hips into his. His friends make some lewd noises, and Joey says, "You can use my back seat if you want."

I pull away from him a little, but his grip is tight, my face is hot with embarrassment. I expect Cal to apologize for putting a kiss like that on display for his friends, but instead he says, "We might be able to manage it in five minutes." He buries his face in my neck as his friends all chuckle. "Cuz she's my little red corvette." I don't know if his friends know the reference to the Prince song, but I do, and I don't appreciate it.

"I've got to go back," I say quietly. "I'll see you tomorrow."

I practically run back to the Pansy. That sure wasn't worth the extra work. I'm so embarrassed. But maybe I'm overreacting. All guys like to show off their girlfriends. Especially when their friends don't have one. He was just trying to make them jealous. Show them up a little.

I just…

Why didn't his face light up when he saw me? He acted so indifferent. Like it hadn't been three weeks. And then that kiss wasn't about being happy to see me either. Must have been the beer. Unless…he doesn't really love me.

"Was he already gone?" Nathan asks.

I'm getting the vacuum out of the walk-in supply closet, and he's there for the Ziploc bags. I'm so lost in thought that his question doesn't register. "Huh?"

"Calvin? The guy you practically floated out of here to see. Was he already gone?"

"No. He was there." I jerk on the vacuum handle trying to get it to lean back so I can push the dumb thing, but it won't release.

Nathan steps on the release button for me. "It usually works better when you do that. But better it than me."

"What?" I frown at him, confused.

He smiles. "I'm glad you're taking your anger out on it and not me."

"I'm not angry!" I practically growl the words. Then I realize how ridiculous I sound and a small smile forms on my lips. "Sorry." I push past him with the vacuum.

He steps back with his hands up in surrender, and a big grin on his face. "What'd he do?"

"Not that it's any of your business, but he just made all his friends think that we're sleeping together." I storm out of the closet, sorry that I told him that. Why did I do that anyway? I always seem to be pouring out my issues to him.

I get all my other closing chores done quickly but polishing the brass takes forever. Abdulla is in his office, and I think everyone else is gone until Nathan grabs a cloth out of the polishing kit and starts working the brass at the other end.

"You don't have to do that," I tell him.

"I want to show you something, but I can't until you're done, so I'm just trying to speed things up."

"Show me what?"

He smiles. "You'll see."

With two, the job gets done quickly, and I put the stuff away and wash my hands.

Nathan waits by the door with his jacket on.

"It's outside?" I ask.

He nods, and I get my purse and put on my jacket too. I knock on Abdulla's door. "We're done. See you Monday," I say loudly enough for him to hear through it. He opens the door from his chair and points to the phone in his other hand, then nods and waves.

"Put your purse in your car," Nathan says. He walks with me to my car and waits while I throw in my purse and re-lock it. "This way," he says.

I follow him, unable to imagine what he's going to show me, especially when we go around the side of the building to the back. The dumpsters are back there with a pretty little white picket fence around them and enough room for the truck that empties them to get in and out, but nothing else. The only parking is in the front, and the main road is to the side. Beyond the dumpsters there's a drainage ditch, a chain-link fence, and then a car dealership that faces the main road. I've actually never been back here. The girls don't have to take out the trash.

"Um, I've seen dumpsters before. I'm assuming that's not it."

"You're not scared of heights, are you?" he asks as he starts to climb a ladder that's attached to the building.

"No. It's on the roof?" I climb up behind him.

He reaches for my hand and helps me navigate the top steps that curve over and down to the roof. "It *is* the roof. Sometimes the guys come up here and hang out."

I look around. There are folding chairs and a little round table. There's even a broken down grill with no legs, resting on some rocks. "I've been working here for two years, and I've never heard about this. You've been here two months and know all about it."

"I'm probably breaking some pizza guy rules bringing you up here. They didn't specifically tell me it was guys only, but it was implied." He walks over to one of the chairs that holds a trash bag and pulls a sleeping bag out of it. He unzips it completely and spreads it out on the ground. "It's such a clear night I wanted to look at the stars. I thought maybe since you were upset, it would make you feel better."

I hesitate. He must be able to tell that the whole situation makes me uncomfortable. It's such a sweet thing, but it's also kind of romantic. And it doesn't feel like he's faking anymore. The guarded looks have been gone for a while.

"No ulterior motives. I promise. I just thought it would make you feel better." He lies down on the sleeping bag as far to the edge as he can get, leaving plenty of room for me.

I decide it *would* make me feel better and lie down close to the other edge. There's almost two feet between us, but I'm still a little tense.

He points out the Big and Little Dipper. I locate Orion's belt and start to relax. It's been a long day, and I'm really tired. I close my eyes. "It is not in the stars to hold our destiny but in ourselves."

"Shakespeare again?"

"Yeah." I hear a car start up in the parking lot below. It's probably Abdulla leaving. I check the time on my cell. Eleven forty-five.

"What's up with that anyway?" He sits up and studies me.

"I don't know. I just love the way it sounds, the cadence of iambic pentameter, the old English. It's genius. The summer I was fifteen I read all his plays, and I wrote down my favorite quotes. I started printing them out, and now I've got them memorized." I shrug and sit up, too.

"I've always struggled to understand his plays. But I like your one-liners. I can get those." He smiles at me and tilts his head. "And I guess they are kind of beautiful."

I look away as I feel a blush starting to creep up my face. "I'm definitely going to fall asleep in church tomorrow," I say.

He laughs. "Yeah. Me too. We always go to the early service."

We are still and quiet for a few more minutes, and then I wrap my arms around my knees. "I'm kind of embarrassed that I told you that before, about Cal." I look over at him, but his eyes are on the sky. "You're so easy to talk to."

His silence feels safe. I lower my voice. "Sophie hates Calvin, so I can't talk to her about him." I sigh. "It just seems like I'm the only person in the world that thinks waiting for marriage is important. I mean, I love him, so why wait?" I feel like I'm just talking to myself, or the darkness, which is thick on the roof. It surrounds me so completely that I feel protected by it. Like I could tell it anything. But even so, I can't speak the other words in my head. The doubts about Cal's feelings for me.

"I guess his friends think we're sleeping together. That's not a big deal though, right? It doesn't matter if they think that. It's not like they're going to spread rumors about me or something. And I'm glad they won't be teasing us about not doing it anymore." The look on Cal's face, like he was too cool to show that he was happy to see me, won't get out of my head. "I don't know why it bothers me so much."

"Because he should protect your honor and your reputation, especially with his friends."

Nathan's voice actually startles me; I was so deep in my own head. Now I'm even more embarrassed. I bury my face in my knees. How did this happen? I'm alone on the roof with an old boyfriend talking about having sex with my current boyfriend.

What is wrong with me?

I jump up and run for the ladder. "Madison, wait." I stop at the rails but keep my back to him. "I don't like Calvin either, so maybe I'm not the best person to say anything. But I'm glad you think I'm easy to talk to. So you can. Talk to me, that is. That's what friends are for."

Is that what we are?

I have to turn around to climb down, and when I do, he's right there. "And do you want to know what I think about," he looks down at his feet, "the sex thing?"

"Um, if you want to tell me."

He runs a hand through his hair. "I think it's good to wait. I'm going to." He sort of peeks up at me, like he's afraid of what my reaction's going to be. When I don't respond he says, "I believe it should be saved for marriage."

His sincerity shines from his eyes, and I smile. "Thanks for bringing me up here."

"Don't tell the other pizza guys."

I shake my head. "I won't." I watch him walk back and pick up the sleeping bag before I climb down the ladder.

A verse comes to me in the shower this time. I scribble it on the back of a sticky note on the bathroom mirror that has a Shakespeare quote on it as soon as I get out.

> *Holding too tight*
> *But I can't loosen my grip.*
> *I've lost the right.*
> *All in this time.*
> *It's much too tight,*
> *A stranglehold.*
> *I can't breathe*
> *Unless I don't look*
> *Back*
> *And hold too tight.*

I try to read it, decipher it, find a reason why it feels so good to get it out of my head, but my hair drips on it, and it becomes illegible in spots. I toss it in the trash.

Chapter Twelve

After church, I change into some jeans and a dressy top. Cal called during church and left a voicemail about plans for the day. My mom passes me in the hall, dressed for yard work. She and Dad are going to rake the leaves and put them in the garden.

"You look nice. Where are you off to?" she asks.

"Cal and I are going to his mom's for lunch."

"He's in town? Why didn't he come to church with us?"

"He wanted to go to his own church—see his friends." I'm glad I'm inside, so I don't get struck by lightning for such a bald-faced lie. But when we started dating, the first thing she asked was if he was a Christian. I lied then, too.

"Is he picking you up?"

"No. He doesn't have his car with him. I'm going to get him."

She gets a strange look on her face. "You're pretty serious about this boy, aren't you?"

I nod. I'm a little nervous about where this is going. We've already had the awkward sex talk, but it was a long time ago.

"Let me give you a little tip about boys." She looks around like she's afraid there are lots of boys around ready to hear her secret. But my dad is in the kitchen, so it's just us. "The way a boy treats his mother is very indicative of how he will treat his wife someday." She looks smug, like she's just shared the secret of the universe with me. "If you're serious about this boy, watch him. The relationship between a boy and his mother is very complicated. But that's how he learns to relate to women, and really, how to treat them."

I think about that on the drive to pick up Cal. It seems a little Freudian. Could it be true?

Cal hops in and gives me a quick kiss. We drive to his mom's apartment near Nashville. We have about two hours until I need to take him to meet his ride back to school. He doesn't say anything about his behavior last night.

I'm still a little mad so I say, "I'd appreciate it if, in the future, you wouldn't kiss me like that in front of your friends."

"What's the big deal?"

"It embarrassed me. Then you practically called me easy."

"What? I did not."

"Your little red corvette? What else could that mean?"

He rolls his eyes. "I didn't mean it like that. I just meant you were hot. I was just trying to make the guys jealous. Losers. None of them have girlfriends." He puts his hand on my leg. "I'm sorry you got embarrassed, but I think that's an overreaction. Besides, it's been a while. I really missed you." He rubs my leg. "And you are so fine. In fact, maybe we should find a place to pull over."

I put my hand on top of his and squeeze. "We're already late."

"She won't care." He unbuckles and leans over the console to kiss my neck.

"Cal! I'm trying to drive. Get back over there."

"I can't help it, Mads. It makes me crazy to be this close to you."

"We are not stopping. You're just going to have to, you know, calm down."

He gives this loud, angry sigh. "I don't know how much longer I can wait."

I'm so stunned that it takes me a minute to respond. "What are you saying? You're going to break up with me if I don't sleep with you?"

He looks out the window. "I don't know."

"That's a great way to show me you love me."

There is only the sound of our breathing in the car for the next few minutes. If he doesn't apologize, I'm dropping him off at his mom's and going home. He can hitch back to school for all I care.

We turn into the apartment complex.

"You're right," he says softly. "I'm sorry. Sometimes I just lose my mind when I think about being with you. It's your fault for being so hot." He grins.

I pull into a parking space and turn off the car. I rest my head on the steering wheel. "It seems like that's all you think about now. We never used to fight, but now we're always fighting about this. Maybe we *should* break up. If sex is so important to you, then you should find someone who doesn't want to wait for marriage."

He reaches over and pulls me as close as he can, wrapping his arms around me. I'm trying really hard not to cry.

"I don't want to be with anyone else. I love you. I'm sorry I said that before. I didn't mean it. We can wait until you're ready. I promise I won't push anymore." He pulls back and lifts up my chin and kisses me gently and my insides prickle with desire. "I promise."

I really, really want to believe him.

He holds my hand as we climb the stairs to his mom's apartment. I haven't seen her since the summer. Circles under her eyes tell me how stressed she is. I guess it's been hard on her trying to make ends meet on her own. She's a few inches shorter than me and has short, blonde, styled hair.

After she makes a big fuss over Cal, she turns to me and gives me a hug. "I'm so glad I get to feed you. You are just skin and bones. Don't you eat?"

"I'm just dancing a lot. Did Cal tell you that I'm in *The Nutcracker*?"

She looks over at him with a mock glare. "I don't think he mentioned that." She swats his arm playfully. "He should have. He never tells me anything anymore."

I glance at the beautifully set table. The food smells amazing. "I'm sorry we're late. The preacher was a little long-winded today."

"You're not late, it's fine. Come on and sit down. Everything's still hot."

We have a feast of ham, mashed potatoes, green bean casserole and corn bread. My mom and dad are always on a diet, so I'm used to lean chicken breasts and salad. That's probably why I pig out whenever I'm away from home. I eat so much it feels like Thanksgiving, which reminds me that that will be the next time I see Cal.

"Do you have any plans for Thanksgiving?" I ask.

"Not really," she says. "My kids are so busy with their own lives.

I was hoping Cal would stay here on his break, though." She looks at him hopefully.

"Sure. If you want. But I may have to borrow your car to drive all the way to Madison's from here. If I can get another lift from school like I did this time, it's a lot cheaper than driving myself and putting all those miles on my car."

She beams at him. "That's not a problem. You may need to drop me at work, though. Busy weekend for retail."

I take my plate to the sink, but Calvin just hands his plate to his mom with a "thank you" and goes into the living room. I help her clear the rest of the table and ask what else I can do, but she waves me away saying she'll deal with it later.

We sit and talk a little while. She tells us that she's been working as a designer for a real estate company for their show homes, and she's also working at a fabric store in a nearby mall.

"I didn't know you were a designer and a seamstress. I only know how to sew practice flags and ribbons on my pointe shoes. Last time I used Mom's sewing machine, the bobbin thread got all tangled up. It was a disaster. I think it hates me."

"I studied design in college, but I never used my degree, except for homemaking. I always wanted to have a little window treatment design shop out of our home when the kids were little, but Cal's father never thought it was worth the trouble."

"The window treatments in your old house are beautiful. I didn't know you made them."

"She's quite the seamstress, aren't you, Mom?" Cal says, his lip curled. I look at him curiously.

"Calvin hated that I made a lot of his clothes for him. But it saved tons of money back before his dad became successful," she explains.

"Speaking of money. Can you spare a few dollars for a poor college student?" He gives her an angelic smile and holds out a hand. "We have to go meet my ride."

"Is it time already?" she asks as she goes and gets her purse. She gives him a couple of twenties, and he gives her a big hug. I put my jacket back on and get my purse.

"Thanks, Mom, you're a lifesaver. Lunch was excellent. I'll see you on Thanksgiving break."

"Thank you so much for having me," I say. "It was great catching up with you, and I really enjoyed the lunch. I feel bad about leaving you with the mess, though."

"She loves it. Don't you Mom?" Calvin drapes an arm around her. "It makes her feel needed."

She laughs and pats his chest. "I wouldn't go so far as to say I love it, but I see you so rarely that I don't mind."

When we're in the car I say, "I was trying to give your mom a compliment about the drapes, but you ruined it with your little sarcastic remark."

"It was more a snide tone than sarcasm. She actually is a good seamstress." I frown at him. He sighs. "The woman named me Calvin during the height of the Calvin and Hobbes popularity and then made me dress in homemade clothes—some even had little tigers on them. How do you think that went over with the bullies on the playgrounds and locker rooms of my childhood?"

"Still, it was mean of you to say that."

"She knew I was just giving her a hard time. She doesn't take me as seriously as you."

"What do you mean by that?"

"I mean," he reaches over and takes my hand, "let's not make a big deal out of it. I don't want to argue with you for the last twenty minutes that I get to see you for two and half weeks."

"I don't want to argue either." I'm quiet for a minute, but then I have to say, "I can't believe you took so much money from her when she's obviously struggling."

He laughs. "Are you sure you don't want to argue?" I scowl at him. "I didn't tell her how much to give me. And forty dollars is not that much."

We get to the meeting spot a little early, so we climb into the backseat. Cal slides over and puts his arm around me. In a very good imitation of Rhett Butler he says, "May I be so bold as to kiss you goodbye?" He even has one eyebrow up and the other down. I love it when he does that—and he knows it.

I giggle and nod. We kiss until I'm ready to rip my clothes off. I've got to be more careful. A horn blows signaling his ride has arrived. God's timing?

"I miss you already," he says, running the back of his hand down my cheek. "I hate school. It's so lonely." The horn blows again, and Cal flips the driver a bird.

I put my arms around him and squeeze. "I love you," I whisper.

He speaks my favorite words into my ear. "I love you, too.

I watch them drive away, a smile lingering on my face. We're just so good together. Too good. I need to be more careful. But he says he won't push anymore. He promised. And he says he loves me. These things swirl around in my head on my way home. But competing for my attention are the words my mom said. *The way a boy treats his mother is very indicative of how he'll treat his wife someday.* And what Sophie said. *You may end up taking care of him the rest of his life.*

If I can't have Cal *and* dance, and I choose Cal over dancing professionally, am I going to end up like his mother someday? Unfulfilled. Divorced. Lonely. Suddenly the fall chill in the air feels like the icy grip of winter. But even putting the heater on high doesn't stop my shivering.

Chapter Thirteen

$\mathcal{D}$uring the down time between shifts, I see Nathan furiously texting with a frown on his face. I walk over to him and pop a mushroom in my mouth. Being a friend works both ways, and I want him to know he can talk to me too.

"Trouble in paradise?"

"Yeah. No. Maybe." He chuckles and takes his Pansy Pizza hat off, rubs his forehead and puts it back on. "She gets mad because I'm so busy." He shrugs. "Can't do much about it."

"At least your busyness is productive. It's not like you're playing games online." *Like some people I know,* I think but would never say out loud. Especially since he's already admitted to not liking Cal. But honestly, I would be thrilled if Cal worked two jobs, volunteered with a cub scout troop, and still managed to make good grades. Candace doesn't know how good she's got it.

He laughs. "I squeeze a little of that in sometimes. Not so much now that I'm trying to make time for her, though."

The way he says that is so sweet, and he's got this look on his face. "Do you love her?" I can't believe the words came out of my mouth. "I'm sorry," I say as I feel my face turn red. "You don't have to answer that. I just—I don't know." I walk away quickly and start rolling silverware.

But the forks and knives are a big blur.

All I see is the school gym. All I feel is Nathan's hand around mine as we walked out to the concession stand from the basketball game. Then his eyes as he pulled me under the bleachers and looked at me with such intensity.

"I love you, Madison Beth Ragland," he said and kissed me.

My heart breaks a little at the memory. My life would have

taken such a different path if I hadn't been such an idiot in ninth grade.

He walks over; a hint of a smile is playing on his lips. "If we can talk about your sex life, it's only fair that you can ask me a personal question." I glance around to make sure no one heard that. "I don't throw that word around lightly. We've only been dating a couple months." His face is all serious. "We don't really agree on a lot of issues."

"Like what? Hunting? I'd have to side with Candace on that one."

"No. She doesn't care about that."

"Your music? Not a big fan of country either."

"I'm talking about big picture things. She practically raised her little sister, so she's not really interested in having kids someday. And she wants to be a corporate lawyer and live in an apartment in a big city like New York. I would hate that."

"Wow. She must be smart."

"She is. And she's a Christian, which is really important to me."

"And she's gorgeous."

He goes back to the kitchen but turns to give me a smile. "There's that."

Big picture issues. Calvin and I tend to avoid those. Just like I avoid telling him that I want to dance. I've got to stop being such a chicken. Nathan and Candace have only been together for a couple months and they've already discussed these things.

Cal and I have talked about going to college together. Him going to med school. Me being a teacher. Probably in his mind we are on the same page. It's really not fair of me to not talk about it. But what if I'm not good enough? How do I justify it?

Do I let it go if he won't support me? Can I?

Then it occurs to me that Cal's never seen me dance. I make a deal with myself. I'll tell him after he watches my performance in *The Nutcracker*. Then he'll see how serious I am. Then he'll get why it means so much to me. That will make all the difference.

I invite Cal to eat Thanksgiving dinner with my family. His family had a tradition of going out for Thanksgiving. Since his parents divorced, they aren't celebrating at all this year.

When he arrives, I introduce him to my sister and Derrick and Kaitlyn. My dad puts on REO Speedwagon for background music and offers everyone a glass of wine while we're waiting for the rolls to finish cooking. He gives me about a quarter of a glass.

"I'd prefer a beer if you have it," Calvin says. My dad gives me a look but goes and gets him a beer. I can't wait for the conversation about why my nineteen-year-old boyfriend already knows that he prefers beer. I elbow Calvin in the ribs, but he's oblivious. He downs the beer in about four gulps; before we even sit down to eat. Kayleigh is trying not to smile, because she knows what Dad's going to say too.

"Calvin's on full scholarship at UT," I say, hoping his accomplishments will cover up for his downing that beer so fast. "He's considering pre-med."

My dad smiles like he's humoring me. "You don't say?"

"Well, not anymore," Calvin says, and I nearly spit my little sip of wine on the floor. "The thought of four extra years of school isn't very appealing, but I'm not exactly sure what I'll do with a degree in Biology. Maybe research."

I stare at him as if he's just grown another head. Looks like he's been keeping big picture issues from me too.

Thankfully, it's time to sit down at the table. We hold hands and my dad says grace. Cal squeezes my hand before we let go. I say an extra prayer that he doesn't mention his beliefs—or rather, lack of them.

Kaitlyn keeps us pretty entertained throughout dinner. At one point, she grabs a stick of butter and tries to eat it. And for some reason, she thinks cranberry sauce is funny. Her giggles crack me up.

After dinner, Cal and I go downstairs to the den to watch *Miracle on 34th Street*, which is a Thanksgiving tradition of mine.

Cal pulls me down on the couch into his lap. "I'm glad to have you to myself. That was *The Kaitlyn Show* up there. You people practically worship that kid."

"She's adorable."

"If you say so."

This makes me a little mad, which reminds me about the beer and the not-going-to-be-a-doctor bombshell. "Did you think asking my dad for a beer was a way to get on his good side? Because it's not."

"He offered."

"No. He politely included us in the wine offer and wouldn't have given you more than me, which wasn't much, because we're underage." I cross my arms on my chest. "I hope he forgets, or I'll be hearing about it later."

He rolls his eyes. "He'd really get mad about that? It was just one beer. Good thing I didn't ask for another one."

I shake my head. "And thanks for telling me you don't want to be a doctor anymore." It's not really fair of me to say that, considering, but I go there anyway.

He hugs me to him and kisses my neck. "Uh huh, I knew you just wanted to marry a doctor." He tickles me, and I giggle and push him away.

"I don't care what you do as long as you're happy."

"As long as we're happy," he corrects. "I wouldn't be happy without you."

Again, he says the perfect thing, so I can't stay mad at him. The boy's got skills. I take a deep breath. "What if I told you I'd rather be a dancer than a teacher?"

"I'd say, you could do both." Before I can argue, he starts kissing me and things get so hot that I totally forget what I was going to say anyway.

I stop by his mom's place on Friday and Saturday before rehearsal, and then we spend a few hours together on Sunday before he goes back. I don't bring up dancing again. Maybe I *could* do both. Maybe I could be in the company and work toward my teaching certificate at Bellmeade. It is one of the major options. It would take a little longer, but when I graduated, I would have been dancing for five or six years. I could marry Cal, teach school, and maybe coach a dance team. That seems like a hybrid plan that would work.

If our relationship can withstand never seeing each other.

Cal was probably thinking that doing both meant my dancing on the UT dance team or at a Knoxville dance studio while I get my teaching certificate. Could I live with that? There are probably some small dance groups I could join.

I picture the company dancers that I watch at every rehearsal and my heart swells with longing.

Maybe not.

Sleep eludes me for a long time. I guess writing poetry is better than staring at the clock, watching the numbers change. It soothes me.

> *I'll stay in the shallows.*
> *The sharks here have had their fill*
> *Of me.*
> *The white picket fence*
> *Is in sight,*
> *a comfort, an anchor,*
> *But the waves lift and twirl me*
> *To face the deep.*
> *The sunrise leaves me breathless.*
> *It pulls like a riptide.*
> *The deeper I go*
> *The more I fear*
> *Being lost at sea.*

Chapter Fourteen

In homeroom, Sophie is a wreck. She looks like she cried all weekend. But she didn't call me or text me or anything, so maybe she's just sick.

I sit in the seat next to her before the bell rings. "What's wrong?"

She looks at me like her heart is broken. I've seen that look before. "Everything," she admits, her eyes shiny with tears.

"What happened?"

"I'm grounded for life. No phone. No computer. But worst of all, no Tim." She puts her head in her hands.

"Sophie? Why?" But the bell rings, and I have to go to my assigned seat. Ken storms in after the bell and doesn't look at anyone. I guess Sophie's not the only one that had a bad weekend.

She gets away before I can question her further, so I have to wait until English.

"Spill," I say as soon as she sits down. Dr. Northcutt is writing a rhyme scheme on the board. It looks like we're starting Shakespearean sonnets, but I can't even be excited with Sophie so upset.

She shakes her head. "We don't have time. I'll write a note." She pulls out a piece of paper and starts to write then wads it up and shoves it in her backpack. "I'll tell you after."

After class, she walks with me to my car and even though she's skipping lunch, and I'm going to be late for work, I just wait.

"Friday night, Tim's parents had a big family party—Mexican themed—and there was a big margarita dispenser. No one was watching it, and I like margaritas, but I drank too much. Way too much. More than I ever have before. Tim did too." She rubs her face. "Everyone was lit. No one even noticed." She takes a deep breath. "We started kissing on the couch. But then, I was feeling sick and went to the bathroom, where I puked my guts out." She shakes her head. "So gross. Never drinking again. When I came back out, my parents were there, yelling at him and asking him where I was."

"Oh, no. Why did they come? Did his parents invite them?"

"Apparently, my Aunt Kristy was there, and she saw us and called them."

My eyes grow wide. "Yikes."

She nods. "Yeah. It was…" She closes her eyes. "After my mom yelled at us, she hunted down his parents and yelled at them. Then my dad said we couldn't see each other anymore. Tim's grounded too. We haven't even talked since then. And I couldn't talk to you either since they took my phone."

Her eyes fill with tears again, but she blinks them back. I've only seen her cry, like, three times in the six years we've been best friends. And once was when she broke her arm, so it doesn't really count. I put my arms around her. "I'm so sorry."

"Can I call him on your phone?"

"Of course." I hand her my phone. While they're talking—he's got lunch at the same time—I duck down in my back seat and change clothes like I'm changing costumes with one number between dances. I pull my hair back into a ponytail as I walk back to her.

She hands me the phone looking much more like herself. "You're a lifesaver. I know you're late. Come early tomorrow, so we can talk."

"Okay." I give her another quick hug and rush to work. When I arrive, Abdulla gives me the evil eye, and I try to look contrite. After the lunch rush and Laurie has gone home, Abdulla lets me have it.

He's got his hands on his hips. "You will stay until after the dinner rush to make up for that."

"I'm sorry, but I can't. I've got rehearsal in Nashville. I barely make it on time as it is."

He mumbles something in Arabic. "Boo hoo. You can be late for me, but not for them? No deal."

"Abdulla," I whine. "I can't be late for rehearsal."

"Fine. Then you come back and help close after rehearsal."

Now I won't have time for my homework, but I nod. "Yes, sir." Maybe I can compose my Shakespearean sonnet as I drive.

I'm making Clam Chowder for the dinner rush and the smell is grossing me out. Nathan walks by with a dark look on his face. Mine probably looks the same. Is *everyone* having a bad day?

"Hey," I say.

He narrows his eyes at me, but says, "Hey." Then he grunts and stomps away.

I follow him into the kitchen. "What's wrong? You're not mad because I was late, are you? Sophie had a meltdown and…"

He looks surprised. "You don't know, do you?"

"What?"

He shakes his head. "I can't believe he didn't tell you."

"Who? Abdulla? Tell me what?"

"Your boyfriend is a piece of work. I've got a strike because of him."

Strikes are red marks on our work record. Three strikes and you're fired. But what does that have to do with Calvin? I can't even put that together in my head. "What?"

"Unbelievable." He pushes through the swinging door. I'm about to follow him, but then I remember the stinky soup. I go back and finish it as quickly as I can then go looking for him. But he's nowhere.

Crud.

I check my phone. Nothing. Cal hasn't texted me all day. And he didn't text or call when he got back to school last night like I asked him to. I had to drop him off here to meet his ride. I didn't even know they came inside. What did he do to get Nathan in trouble? I text Cal, asking what happened. After five minutes with no response, I hunt down Rick Lester.

Rick's an assistant manager now and always knows everything that's going on. I usually try to avoid him since he kissed me in the dining room one night when we were closing. He asked me out, but with his fast hands I knew I'd be in over my head. There isn't a girl at the Pansy that hasn't had his hands on her at some point—and usually not by choice.

"Do you know why Nathan's mad at me?" I ask him.

He grins as he pulls a sack of flour out of the pantry. "Because your crappy boyfriend got him in trouble."

Why does everyone hate Calvin? "When did that happen?" I lean against the counter so he can't get behind me.

"Last night. He came in with Brett Barnes. What a pair."

"He's not friends with him, really. He just got a ride home from him a couple of times."

He laughs. "Yeah. Well, Brett doesn't have friends. He has customers."

"What do you mean?"

"He was a dealer in high school. I don't suppose he's changed."

Great. "So, what happened last night?"

"Calvin was talking smack about you. And Nathan told him to zip it. But he got all up in his face, so Nathan decided to beat that smack out of him."

I draw in a sharp breath. "What? Is he all right?"

"I happened to be nearby, so I pulled Nathan off him, not for his sake, though. Nathan only got one good punch in, and Calvin folded like a deck of cards. It was sweet."

"How can you say that?"

"I heard what he said."

"About me? What?"

He moves in close, resting his wrist on my shoulder. "Are you sure you want to know? Course it could be true. I don't know." His eyes move up and down my body.

I cross my arms over my chest. I can't back away, and he knows it. "I doubt it. Tell me."

"There was some old song on the radio about somebody wanting to dance. And Brett said something about you being a dancer and how he heard dancers were good. And Calvin says, 'Dancers do it in all positions.' And they laughed. Calvin told him you were always begging for it and could never get enough. That's when Nathan stepped in. He said you were his friend, and he didn't think you would like them talking about you like that. And Calvin got all possessive. No one else was in here, or Abdulla would have really freaked."

I put my hands over my face. Anger and embarrassment cause tears to threaten as I walk back to the kitchen. I take a few deep breaths. Am I overreacting? *Talking smack,* Rick said. I guess he was just trying to look good in front of this Brett guy.

Who may be a drug dealer.

Kill. Me. Now.

Nathan finally comes back as I'm getting my stuff together to leave. I can't even look at him. "Rick told me. I'm sorry."

"What are *you* apologizing for?"

"You did that for me. It was my boyfriend, so it was my fault you got the strike. I'm really sorry."

He shakes his head. "It wasn't your fault."

I can feel his eyes on me as I get my timecard and punch out.

"Just tell me you're going to break up with that jerk."

I sigh. "He only acts that way around his friends. He's totally different around me. I don't know how to feel about it. I'm really mad at him, and kind of hurt, and embarrassed. Really embarrassed. Rick was looking at me like…" I close my eyes and shake off those thoughts. But…" I shrug. "I love him. So I have to find a way to forgive him, right? Forgiveness is part of love."

He looks murderous again but doesn't say anything. He walks away, but I stop him. "Nathan?" I hope he can forgive me for forgiving Cal. "Um…thanks for defending me."

I think his look softens a little, but maybe it's wishful thinking, then he nods.

When I get home from closing. I'm so exhausted I can hardly think straight, but I have to yell at Calvin. If I don't get this anger off my chest, I'll never get to sleep. No matter how tired I am.

I'm shocked to find a text from Cal that must've come during my drive home. But it's not an apology or an explanation. It's a jealous rant that begins with:

> *Who is Nathan?*

My hands are shaking as I type a reply.

> *Oh no. You are not going to turn this around on me. There is nothing going on between me and Nathan. How can you even accuse*

> *me of that?!! You are the one at fault here.*
> *"Dancers do it in all positions." ??? "She was*
> *begging for it." ??? WTH?? And Brett is a*
> *drug dealer??!!!*
> *I am so upset there are no words. Don't*
> *bother trying to come home next weekend.*
> *I don't want to see you. I'm not sure I ever*
> *want to see you again.*

He calls, but I turn off my phone. It didn't really make me feel better like I thought it would. I toss and turn all night wondering if I really meant that last bit.

True love forgives.

Shouldn't I be willing to forgive this little personality flaw? He wants the approval of his friends. Everyone does. If I break up with him, wouldn't it be more because I want the approval of my friends than because I don't love him anymore? I do love him. I get him. We have loads of stuff in common. We're so happy when we're together, just the two of us. I think I want to spend the rest of my life with him. God has put me in his life for a reason. I know he's going to be a Christian someday.

Besides, I've done worse. It's not like he cheated on me.

He wasn't trying to hurt me with that *smack talk*, as Rick called it. No one was around. He never expected it to get back to me. He certainly never expected to get punched for it. It almost makes me feel sorry for him. Almost. Nathan is strong. Calvin is…not.

Still…

It wasn't honorable. Nathan's words come back to me: *he should protect your honor and your reputation.*

Maybe he doesn't really love me. Somehow it always circles back to that.

And my brain won't let me sleep until I write down the poetry floating around in it. That makes me feel better than yelling at Cal in that text. But the meaning is all too clear this time. I don't know how long I can keep burying my head in the sand, pretending that Cal loves me as much as I love him.

Look, but don't see

Happily Ever After
Will be mine
As long as I let it be
Trust the prince
White horse and
All that
Will be mine
for the low, low price
Of ignorance.

Chapter Fifteen

I wait in the parking lot for Sophie Tuesday morning. I tell her what Cal said, and she is livid.

"This is what I'm talking about. A complete lack of respect."

"It's just a guy thing. He likes to brag—"

"It's not bragging if it's lies. It's lying."

I sigh. "But is it really a big deal for him to lie to look like a big shot to his friends? There's no real harm done. Maybe I just should accept that he has a need to look superior," I say. "Hence the bragging, and the condescending tone. Everyone has personality flaws. If I love him, I should forgive him."

"That sounds like settling to me. You should never settle. There are guys out there that aren't conceited, needy jerks. Look at Nathan."

Is it settling or just looking past his flaws to who he really is?

"Nathan's an exception. But guys like him are few and far between, and they're usually taken. It's probably just a phase—being so sex-obsessed, I mean. Deep down, Calvin is a good guy who occasionally exhibits bad behavior. It's not like I'm a saint. How can I judge him for it?"

Sophie shakes her head. "I wish you could see it from my perspective."

"Enough about me. Any luck with your parents?"

"Well, they've changed grounded forever to after Christmas. But I think that's because my birthday's coming up, and I told them I would move out when I'm eighteen if they continue to be so unreasonable."

"Wow. That's quite a threat. I don't think my parents will go against yours and let you stay with us. Where would you go?"

"I don't know. I haven't thought that far ahead. I don't really want to move out and spend all my college money on an apartment." She rubs her face. "Other than that threat, though, I've been super contrite. The drinking too much was a big mistake—of course, drinking at all is a huge deal to them. And I blamed the PDA on the drinking—which is true. We never would've done that in front of everyone if we hadn't been drunk."

"I'm praying they'll cool off. Weren't they high school sweethearts? They know how it is. Surely, they'll come around."

"From your lips to God's ears. But you know how they are. Swearing, drinking, gambling, lewd dancing, making out on the couch—all worthy of a first-class ticket to hell. They pray for your soul, by the way, since you're on the dance team." She picks up her backpack from the floorboard and pulls her phone from the pocket. "For emergencies only—and they will be checking it. But at least they gave it back. Still… I miss him so much. Now I see how you felt when Cal went to college."

"It's the worst."

"What are you going to do about him?"

"I don't know. I'm pretty mad now, but I also feel kind of sorry for him. He sure wasn't expecting Nathan."

She grins. "Yeah. That was awesome."

I start to object, but she waves her hand. "Sorry. I get it. You've got to follow your heart."

When she says that, my sister's scripture quote hits me hard. *The heart is deceitful above all things…*

Am I supposed to follow my heart?

I hand her my phone. "Here. Give it back in English."

"I love you!" she squeals.

I check my phone obsessively once I get it back from Sophie. At eight-thirty, after *Nutcracker* rehearsal, I finally have two texts from Cal.

> *You can't be serious about not seeing me again.*
> *I'm sure your FRIEND blew the whole thing out*
> *of proportion. We were talking about dancers in*

*general not you specifically anyway. We were
just joking around.*

*I love you, Mads. I didn't mean to hurt you. I'm
really sorry if you took all that the wrong way.*

I'm coming home Saturday to make it up to you.

I call Laurie to see if she'll switch shifts with me, since I'm supposed to work after rehearsal on Saturday. She agrees to give me her Sunday night shift.

"So, I guess you heard about the whole Calvin-Nathan craziness," I ask her.

"Rick made sure everyone heard, until Nathan threatened him too." She laughs.

"He did?" He's probably just tired of hearing about it. Rick is such a blabbermouth.

"What's the deal with you two anyway? It was like Iceland at work yesterday."

"There's no deal. It's just Calvin did something similar a few weeks ago, and I told Nathan how much it upset me, so I guess it just made him mad that he would do it again. It makes me mad too. We haven't even had sex. But he says that his friends just assume, and he doesn't correct them."

"He did it before? Are you going to dump him?"

"No. I love him. He just did a stupid thing. Everybody does stupid things sometimes."

"The same thing? Twice? Sounds like it's not a mistake."

"You don't think I should forgive him?"

"I wouldn't."

"He's so different when it's just us. I can't even imagine him saying those things. It makes it harder for me to stay mad."

"I don't know Calvin, so I don't know what to tell you."

"He says he's going to make it up to me on Saturday. That's why I wanted to switch. I really appreciate it."

"No problem. See you tomorrow."

I find out after dance team practice on Thursday why Ken hasn't been his usual flirty self. We're lying on the floor, completely wiped out. And I'm so glad that I don't have to drag myself to rehearsal after this like I do on Tuesdays.

Chloe gets up and digs a pill bottle out of her bag and pops one in her mouth. She starts swearing like a sailor and shoves her bag away. "I hope his male parts rot and fall off."

"That's harsh. I guess you broke up?"

She lowers her voice to a whisper. "He gave me HPV. The kind with genital warts. He did sleep with Lisa and who knows who else. And now I have to live with this for the rest of my life."

"Didn't you get the vaccination?" My mom didn't think I needed it, since I wasn't sexually active, but most of my friends got it.

"It's a different strain."

"There are different strains?"

She nods. "Hundreds. The vaccine only protects against four."

"*Ewww.* Isn't there some kind of medicine to cure it?"

She shakes her head. "I've got pills to take for the symptoms, but it's viral. There's no cure."

"That's horrible. I'm so sorry."

"It's way past horrible. I was a virgin when we started dating. Now I'm going to have to tell everyone I date that I have this disgusting virus, and they're going to think I was easy in high school." She growls. "I may just swear off guys for the next five years." She chugs her water until there are only a few drops left and then lets it drip on her forehead.

Ken Reynolds. Not so perfect after all. More proof of the reality that guys do stupid things. He cheated deliberately, though. That's the ultimate betrayal of trust. Chloe should break up with him. But me accepting the reality and moving on to a day when Cal grows out of the need to brag, that's not settling. Is it? I don't want to give up on our happily ever after over immature behavior he's going to outgrow.

Ms. Vaughan comes over to us and tells us she'd like to add a solo intro to two of the routines. One with me and one with Chloe.

"Maybe you better give them both to Chloe," I say. "With *The Nutcracker* and everything—" I don't want to tell her that if I start taking daily classes in Nashville in January, I may have to drop dance team.

"You're the best dancer on the team," Chloe says. "Everyone knows it."

I smile. "Not hardly, but thanks for saying so."

"Why don't you both learn the solos then you can take turns at performances," Ms. Vaughan says.

We agree to do it, but I don't know when I'm going to squeeze in extra practice time. I tell them the only time I can work on it will be next Thursday. The Thursday after that is opening night. We also have mid-terms that week. She says that's fine for a start, and we'll finish it up in January. Guilt knots up my stomach, but I keep my mouth shut. Nothing is decided. The scholarship audition is coming up this weekend. I'll wait until after that.

Nathan has been distant and cold all week, like Laurie said: Iceland. Friday is no exception. We both have the short shift today. He decides to eat lunch here. I get a sub sandwich and sit across from him in a booth in the back.

"I've missed you this week," I say as I sit.

He frowns at me. "I'm right here."

"You have every right to be mad at me, I know. I get it. But please don't."

He continues to scowl. "I'm not hungry anymore," he says and starts to leave.

I grab his arm. "Wait. Please." He stops, and I can't bear to look into his eyes. I let go of him and stare at my plate. "What he did was bad, but what I did to you was worse. And I know that I'd do anything to take that back, so I just have to give him the benefit of the doubt when he tells me that he didn't mean to hurt me, and that he loves me." I pick up a potato chip and dip it in the sandwich sauce. "I just have to."

"You still haven't forgiven yourself for that." It's not a question.

I shrug and eat the chip, afraid to look and see if he's still scowling. He hasn't left, so I take that as a good sign. "Nathan, I really value your friendship. Please don't be mad at me. I can't help the way I feel."

"He doesn't deserve you. And he sure doesn't appreciate you."

I take a long sip of my soda, hoping to swallow down the sick feeling at the thought of Nathan hating me again. "Maybe I don't deserve him."

"No. You deserve better, but I don't know what else to say to make you believe that."

"So will you stop giving me the cold shoulder?"

"If you'll do me a favor." I nod and finally dare to look at him. "Just try to see Calvin objectively, instead of through this veil of guilt because of something stupid you did when you were fourteen."

I'm not sure I know how to do that. "I'll try," I say, and I must sound sincere because he almost smiles.

I'm so nervous about the date, I don't do my best at rehearsal. I shower and put on my favorite dress when I get home. Calvin picks me up in his freshly detailed Nissan Sentra, and we go to my favorite Japanese restaurant where they cook the food in front of you. I haven't been treated like this since our Valentine's date last year. That ended in me telling him I loved him, him not saying it back, and his breaking up with me a week later. But that was then. I try to focus on now, even though it makes me miss the way he treated me the first time we dated. Fancy restaurants, flowers, candy.

Stop being shallow. He is not just dating me because I pay for everything. Just like that is not the reason I dated him the first time. Sophie needs to get out of my head.

The restaurant is crowded, and we wait on a couch for our name to be called. He's all proud of himself for getting a beer with a fake ID.

"You just ruined a great start to a make-it-up-to-me evening," I say. The faint bruising on his cheekbone is a constant reminder to me why we're here, but I guess he's forgotten.

"When are you going to stop being such a goody-goody? It's just beer."

"Oh. Name calling. That's helpful." I cross my arms over my chest.

He puts the beer on the end table. "I was just nervous, okay? I won't drink anymore tonight." He takes my hand and kisses it. "You're right. This evening is all about you. Tell me how rehearsals are going."

He never asks me about dance in our calls, so I tell him about the choreographer and the girl, Tanya, that I share the part with. And then I tell him how I sit in the wings and watch the company dancers, which ones are my favorites—Celeste and Monica—and why.

He's looking at me like he wants to kiss me, and I wonder if he's responding to how passionately I feel about dance. I tell him about opening night and ask him to come.

"You're finished with exams by then, aren't you?"

"When is it again?"

"Thursday after next."

A cloud seems to pass over his face. "Yeah. I'll be done."

"What's wrong?"

"I'm not doing so well in my classes. I really have to ace my finals to keep my scholarship."

Too much gaming and partying, I think, but I can see he's worried, so I don't say it. Instead I say, "You can do it. You'll just have to really buckle down next week."

"If I lose my scholarship—"

I squeeze his hand. "You won't."

"I had it so easy in high school. I never really learned how to study. And the college professors are so strict about attendance. Some of them make it count as a grade which is so stupid if I can turn in the work on time and show up for tests."

"Why can't you make it to class?"

"I've finally made some friends and there are lots of parties. Not just on weekends. And sometimes I'm in the middle of a game, and I can't leave. They put everything online. It shouldn't be a big deal to skip."

I wonder if Brett Barnes is one of his friends. Is he hung over from drinking, or is he taking drugs too? I thought he was smarter than that.

I keep my thoughts to myself. He needs encouragement not judgment. "Everyone struggles with adjusting their first semester."

He smiles and puts his arm around me. "How would you know?"

"That's what I've heard." Our beeper lights up and starts vibrating. "Yay! I'm starving. Let's go."

Dinner is wonderful. But I bite my tongue several times to keep from asking where he got the money to pay for it. For once, I don't even offer to leave the tip. I've spent tons of money on him in the past six months.

So, why do I feel guilty?

After dinner, he takes me back to his house. We stop and get ice cream for later on the way. He wants to show me this game he loves and how realistic it is. I have to admit that it's an amazing game, but sitting there watching someone else livestream their play gets old after a while. Is this how he would feel watching me dance?

I convince him it's time for ice cream, although I'm still too full from dinner to really enjoy it. We go into the kitchen to eat. I tell him about what happened with Sophie and Tim.

"She's pretty torn up. I don't know what to tell her."

"I'm sure her parents will get over it. Let's go in my room," he says. "All this kissing talk is making me want you."

"You promised." I knew it was too good to be true.

He stands and pulls me up too, kissing my neck and making all my thoughts fuzzy. "I'll keep my promise. There are other things we can do." He pulls on the neck of my sweater and kisses me lower and lower.

My heart is beating a million miles a minute. "I don't know. It seems like *other things* will make it impossible to stop."

"I'll keep my promise," he whispers and tugs me into his room.

When he drives me home, I know I made a mistake, crossed a line. The guilt bites deep. Even though I'm technically still a virgin, I don't feel so virginal anymore. What happened to my ideals of only being that personal with *The One*? They flew out Calvin's bedroom window.

But holy kisses, Batman, it was hot.

Chapter Sixteen

*T*here are only five other girls at the scholarship audition. Four of them are younger than me and don't pose much competition, but the other one is Megan. My heart sinks when I see her. There's no way I can beat her. She's Clara.

Maybe since there are younger girls here, everyone is judged based on the level they are. I'm obviously not at Megan's level, but I'm way above some of these other girls, so it's not very fair for them to compete against me. Still, if it's age-based, I'm sunk.

"Madison, right? The parlor maid?" Megan asks as we put our pointe shoes on.

"That's me. You're doing an amazing job as Clara. How do you manage school, being in both casts?"

"I'm homeschooled. My mom lets it count as school since I've got all my required credits, and I want to dance professionally."

Must be nice to have a supportive mom. "That's helpful."

"Yeah. It's great, but since I can't work for real with all my training, I can't help pay for classes."

I was hoping she'd be snarky and easy to dislike, since she hasn't said a word to me at the theatre. But here I am liking her already. She's not a great arch nemesis.

My mind battles between: *I have to crush her in this audition*, and *I hope she gets the scholarship.*

We move to the barre to warm up. She smiles sweetly. I wonder if she's thinking that I have no chance.

Ms. Turpin and one of my favorite dancers from the company, Celeste, as well as another one of the teachers here that I've seen before, come in through the door at the other end of the massive room. They're all holding clipboards. Celeste and the teacher, I think her name is Ms. Lyndell, sit in folding chairs, while Ms. Turpin glides over to the sound system and starts some music.

I take some deep breaths, trying to push away all my fears and concentrate only on the music and my body. We do a short barre, then some steps across the floor. She has us do leaps and Megan does a Russian instead. Perfectly. Show off.

I didn't know we could do harder stuff than what she asks us to do.

She has us do pirouettes one at a time. I nail a double. *Take that, Miss Russian.* She nails a double too. We do fouetté turns. Megan does five in a row. I do six, but my last one is wobbly.

Then Ms. Turpin says, "Now, I want to get a sense of your range. I want you to do a combination, something short, that's not ballet."

I don't trust myself to improvise, so I use a section of one of our dance team routines. It has an aerial in it. It took me forever to get that aerial, so I'm quite proud of it. That shows them I can do jazz and tumbling too.

Megan does an emotion-filled modern combination. It's lovely, but it doesn't showcase her other dance skills as well as my piece did mine.

The other teacher, Ms. Lyndell, gets up and teaches us a combination. It's really easy, since there are younger ones here. I notice Ms. Turpin writing lots of notes. Celeste just watches. I don't even think she has a pen. Her clipboard is on the floor under her chair. She must have a great memory.

I leave feeling pretty good about it. I did my best. That's all I can do.

Sunday night, I'm humming the music from *Nutcracker* all evening. I can put the audition out of my mind. Our mid-term for English is a poetry notebook that we've been compiling all semester and a research paper on a particular poet. No-brainer who I chose. It's due next week, and then we get them back during the mid-term time. I'm not worried about that or my other exams either. With everything else going on, it's a relief to not be stressing over schoolwork, too.

And last night with Cal was wonderful. The best part is that he planned and paid for the whole thing. It never really bothered me to always be the one that does that, but it sure was nice being treated for a change. And after our make-out session, I feel closer to him than ever. I decided not to be ashamed, because he and I love each other and do want to get married someday. Maybe Sophie is right about it being more about love than marriage. I really felt loved for the first time since he went away to college. Things are definitely back on track.

I do a little twirl with a pizza in hand before I call out on the microphone that the order is ready. Abdulla gives me a frown, but I just shrug and grin. It must be contagious, because he rolls his eyes and tries not to smile.

Sophie comes in with Tim and they're holding hands. I wish I could run around the counter and hug her! "They caved?"

"They caved!" They look at each other with such love. "Short leash. But not grounded."

I ring them up, all of us smiling the whole time.

"So, your make-up date went well?" she asks.

"Yes, thank you. It was amazing."

Nathan walks behind me and sees them. "Sophie," he says and nods. Her eyes bug out, and she looks at me like I owe her an explanation.

"What?" I mouth, but I've got another customer and have to take his order. I feel my phone buzz in my pocket a few minutes later. As soon as I have a chance, I slip into the kitchen to read her text.

Sophie:

> *WTH?! You did not tell me that Nathan grew up into a hottie!!! Dump C and throw yourself at N's feet immediately!!! This is not a request!!*

Me:

> *LOL! He's taken. Besides I just told you C and I made up. : P*

I'd like to remind her that Nathan wouldn't trust me as far as he could throw me, but she probably forgot all about my cheating. She was so wrapped up in Caleb and the fact that we could double, she never saw how miserable I was dating Sean when my heart was still Nathan's. I shove my phone back in my pocket and rush out to the counter to find a line of customers waiting. I look around for Abdulla.

"You got lucky," Nathan's voice says from behind me. "He's on the phone in the office."

I glance at him and smile. He's just come back from busing tables.

That's all I need: Sophie talking to Nathan. I hope that didn't happen, but when Sophie and Tim leave, she's got that look on her face. The one she gets when she's been sticking that cute little button nose in where it doesn't belong.

She bats her eyes in mock innocence. "See you tomorrow."

"What did you do?"

"I don't know what you're talking about."

"Sophie!"

She just wiggles her eyebrows and waltzes right out the door. *Ugh!*

Abdulla locks us in and cranks the radio up. He knows the words to most of the oldies that play and occasionally grabs the microphone that we use to call people up for their orders to sing along. I pas de deux with the vacuum and pirouette around the restaurant. At one point, I catch Nathan's eyes on me, and he's smiling.

"Sophie said you made up with Calvin," he says.

So she *did* talk to him.

"I guess that's why you're in such a good mood."

I don't really want to talk about Calvin with Nathan. I just shrug and do a cabriole holding my dish towel over my head and then laugh at his expression. "I wish I could dance all the time."

"My mom's taking my sister to see *The Nutcracker*. Did you ever talk to your parents about the company?"

I feel the smile slide off my face like rain down a windshield. I shake my head. Calvin's words float across my mind: *You could do both.*

"I'm sorry. Did I hit a nerve?"

Abdulla's voice comes blaring over the mic. It's not even the right words to the song. I roll my eyes.

"It's late. We better finish up and get out of here. Let me know when your sister's coming, and I'll try to get her some autographed shoes."

He looks confused, so I explain. "The company dancers wear out their shoes pretty regularly, so they autograph them and give them to fans."

He crinkles his nose. "Smelly old shoes, huh?"

"I seem to remember a smelly old baseball glove with an autograph on it that meant a lot to you."

"Good point."

I think I've dodged the bullet on the teaching conversation, but after we finish up and walk out to our cars, he brings it up again.

"You should talk to them. You're really talented."

I freeze at his words, and my whole body slumps from the weight of them. He stops beside me.

How can I explain that no one sees how much it means to me?

"I tried to bring up joining the Company with my mom, and she shut me down. She's dead set on my being a teacher. I told my sister, and she was kind of encouraging, but she didn't say much, which usually means she's trying not to hurt my feelings."

He takes my hand and twirls me around. "Ballerina girl, you have to do what makes you happy."

No one sees—but Nathan.

"Maybe I'm not good enough."

"You're good enough to teach." He says it with such certainty. "You've already proven that. If you're not good enough for the Company now, then get good enough."

"I'm trying, but it's not that simple. I auditioned for a scholarship for classes, because I'd have to take classes almost every day to prepare, and it's really expensive. If I get it, then my parents will have to let me, I think. But if I don't—I don't know. If I pay for it myself, it would take all of my savings, and I don't think Abdulla would keep me on if I couldn't ever work nights or Saturdays."

He's looking at me with a frown on his face like he's disappointed in me. He lifts one eyebrow. "Lot of *ifs* in there. You're making excuses. No one is going to support your dream if you don't support it first. You have to approach it like, this is what I want, and this is how I'm going to get it."

I just stare at him. I know he's right, but I don't know how he got so wise. And why is he so nice to me? We may be friends on the surface, but deep down … how could he not still hate me? I completely broke his heart. His young, perfect, great big heart.

"What?" he asks, since I'm staring.

I can't put into words what his support means to me, so I throw my arms around his neck and hug him. Then I apologize and run to my car, a blush crawling up my face.

Chapter Seventeen

"All right. What did you say to Nathan last night?" I ask Sophie before the bell.

Her eyes light up. "Why? Did he say something?"

"Sophie! What did you say?"

She pretends to think about it. "*Hmmm.* Last night … last night, no, can't remember. Sorry."

"He said you told him that I made up with Calvin. What else?"

"I'm drawing a blank." She taps her forehead. "Oldtimers. They say it's a disease of seniors." She laughs. "Get it? We're seniors."

"That's not even funny. You're just being purposely obnoxious. Tell me."

"What I may or may not have said is none of your business, because I didn't say it to you. Why do you care anyway?"

"I can't figure out why he's so nice to me. Especially since he's got to hate me."

"Just because *you* hate you for that whole cheating incident a million years ago, doesn't mean he hates you. Let it go. Be friends. He's a nice guy. You said yourself that he's an exception."

I'm not sure how to respond. I really didn't think she remembered the cheating incident or knew that I still felt awful about it. And I can't understand why she's promoting him as a great best friend when she's already got the job.

"Yes. Yes. I know it's shocking. I can be intuitive sometimes. I just try not to let it show."

I'm still suspicious, but she's pretty stubborn, so I guess I'll never know.

"What about you and Tim? How'd did you get your parents to let you see him again?"

"It was Tim's mom, really. She came over and talked to my mom Saturday and took full responsibility because of the unattended margaritas. So they decided that since I'm an exemplary student and haven't given them a reason to doubt my decisions before—thank goodness, they don't know all my decisions—they would blame my naivety and the alcohol. And we both promised that we would never drink again. Believe me, the puking, the headache, the stupidity … *so* not worth the temporary buzz." The bell rings, and she waves me away.

Rehearsals get more intense leading up to opening night. I'm so exhausted I don't bother to thaw out the meals my mom left for me in the freezer, but slap together peanut butter and jellies instead.

My parents went to Florida to visit my grandparents. They usually go the day after Christmas, but this year my dad has some kind of CPA New Year's Eve party—and I use that word loosely considering it's a Christian accountant's group—so they went before. They'll be back the twentieth so they can come see one of the last *Nutcracker* performances.

I start texting Cal a lot. Even if he doesn't respond, at least I can know that I told him everything I'm feeling. I want to believe that if I pour out my heart to him then he'll get it. He'll understand why dance is so important to me. Sometimes it comes out in poetry.

When it gets closer to opening night, I buy him a ticket that will be waiting for him at the door. Sophie and Tim come Tuesday night to the free full dress rehearsal. They leave after the party scene though, because of exams. It was sweet of them to come at all. Sophie's got three AP classes. I don't know how she keeps up with all the work.

I breeze through my Teaching as a Profession exam, then do okay on Pre-Calculus. I don't think I failed it, but towards the end the numbers started all running together in my head. The other cast has their full dress on Wednesday night, so I get the night off and go to the youth group Christmas party. I score a neon green lava lamp in the white elephant gift exchange and sign up to sing carols next Saturday evening at the local nursing homes.

I have reminded Cal in each of the three short calls this week about opening night. He said he would come. He's really worried about his exams, though, so he barely said anything else.

Thursday morning, I ace my C.E. exam and have thirty minutes to kill before I have to go to Dr. Northcutt's room to get my paper and poetry notebook back. I swing by the guidance office. She's actually here but on the phone. The wall outside the office is covered with pamphlets, some about STDs, one about how to talk to your parents about sex, one about how to come out to your parents. One is titled, *"Four Ways to Tell if You're in an Unhealthy Relationship."*

How could someone not know they were in a bad relationship? I pull it out to see. It lists the danger signs.

1. *Do you get along best when you isolate yourselves from others?*
2. *Do your friends think that you've changed?*
3. *Are you keeping secrets?*
4. *Do either of you exhibit obsessive behavior?*

Before I have time to read the explanations Ms. Richards tells me I can come in. I shove the pamphlet back in its slot and take a seat in front of her desk. It's so tidy, with only a few folders, a phone, a desk calendar and a photograph that I can't see. There are some college banners and motivational posters on the wall. The one with the kitten that says, *Hang in There*, I've seen a million times. Steam comes from the bright yellow mug in front of her that must be hazelnut coffee since the whole room smells like it.

"What can I do for you?" she asks. She isn't very old which helps me feel more comfortable with her for some reason. Like I'm talking to my sister.

No time to mess around, I lay it all out for her: the company, Bellmeade, teaching. All the worries I've kept bottled up pour out on her desk like flat soda. I'm holding my breath in hopes that she has the skills to mop it up for me.

"I'm not sure if I should go ahead and apply to other colleges, in case I don't make it, or if I shouldn't worry about that because if

I don't make it what I really want to do is keep taking classes and try out again until I do."

She looks amused at my outburst. "Okay then. My advice to you would be to definitely go ahead and apply to several colleges with good dance programs. If you don't make it into the company, you may want to go to college where you can major in dance. Lots of the universities have dance companies that might be just as good as City Ballet and offer you the same range of experience."

"The problem is that I don't think my parents will be okay with me majoring in dance."

She nods and takes a sip of her coffee. "And if they're paying for it—"

"Right."

"What I'm hearing, though, is that you're not sure how they're going to react. It might be time to have that conversation." She puts her cup down. "You won't really know how to proceed until you do. Plus, you could audition for a dance scholarship. But only if you hurry up and apply."

"Yeah. I know." I stand, disappointed in her mopping skills. My thought explosion is just dripping down the desk into the cute gray and white striped area rug. "Thanks, anyway."

She stands too. "Good luck."

I just nod and head to English. That was a waste. Nathan basically said the same thing already. What neither one of them did say, though, is *how* to talk to my parents when I'm such a chicken. Or how to tell Cal if my parents are good with it.

At the theatre, everyone is as buzzed as me. The air crackles with excitement, and I can't wait to get on stage. Like always, I dance as if I'll never dance again. I pour my heart into every movement because this is where I truly live. Nothing else matters on stage.

After my part, I stand out of the way but still in the wings, so I can watch the company dancers. There are a handful of little girls that do the same. Ms. Turpin asked me to keep an eye on them and keep them out of the way during rehearsals. She didn't want to keep us from watching, though. She knows that some girls watch and enjoy and go home, and some, like us, are mesmerized. We watch and become a part of it. We're probably not supposed to watch during the actual performance, so I tell the girls to be extra still and quiet.

Celeste actually comes and stands near me when she's finished, just before intermission. She gulps down water, so I hand her a towel, and she looks at me like I appeared out of thin air. She dabs her face lightly with the towel, trying not to remove her stage makeup.

"I love watching you dance," I say. "I hope I can be as good as you someday. I'd love to be in the company."

"God, I need a cigarette," she says. "Whose stupid idea was it to not let us have freaking cigarettes in the theatre?" She looks at my costume. "You're the maid in the party scene."

I nod, amazed that she knows this.

"You auditioned for the scholarship, too." She sighs. "You've got stage presence, but to be honest, you aren't company material. You could work on your turnout and extension—and you should—but you can't do anything about your size. You don't have the right body type for the company. You're too tall and broad-shouldered and look at the size of your feet." She shakes her head, disgusted by my size nines. "It's a shame. You have a dancer's heart, it's just in the wrong body. I didn't vote for you for the scholarship. Clearly, it should go to Megan."

She gives an apologetic shrug and flits away on her tiny, size-six feet leaving me completely unable to move. It's like she cast a spell. I don't blink. I don't even think I'm breathing until the room starts to spin, and I stagger over to a chair and then my breaths come in short gasps.

One of the little girls, Eva, comes over and takes my hand. "Don't cry," she says. I wipe my wet face and stare at her little, black, mouse nose. The rest of the girls crowd around me.

"She was mean," Carly says. I notice her frizzy curls have come out of her bun, again, and I automatically smooth them back.

"She's just jealous 'cause you're better than her." This from Ashley, the oldest of the group at twelve.

I give them a weak smile. "It's intermission. We need to get you out of those costumes."

The spell of paralysis breaks, and I lead them down to the dressing rooms. The girls are free to go after they change since it's so late and a school night. I help them find their parents and feel utterly alone when they're gone. I have to stay for the curtain call. I doubt anyone would miss me if I wasn't there, but this is a professional performance, and I want to be professional.

The words that are stuck on repeat in my brain are: that had to be the sign.

Chapter Eighteen

I have no memory of the drive home but am surprised to find Calvin waiting for me in my driveway holding a bouquet of roses—ballet pink, my favorite.

I run to him and can't believe how comforted I am by his arms around me.

"You were wonderful," he says, presenting me with the roses.

"You came." The heaviness in my heart lightens a little.

"Of course. I left at intermission, though. I looked for you before I left, but the security goons wouldn't let me backstage."

"I was helping the little girls anyway," I say.

He smiles and runs his thumb down my face. "Figures." He looks different, but I don't quite understand why. Something sweeter in his expression?

We go inside and he's acting kind of nervous and shy. I pull the pins out of my hair and brush it out. "I need to shower and get all this stage makeup off," I say.

"Okay. I'll wait in your room."

I get out of the shower and slip into my sweats. Soft music plays from Cal's phone and all the candles in my room are lit.

Wow.

Cal pulls me to sit on the bed. "I want to… Can I give you your Christmas present now?" Again, he seems shy and uncertain. I've never seen this side of him, except maybe when he showed up at dance camp.

"Okay."

He hands me a small ring-sized box. My heart starts pounding a mile a minute as I start to freak out. Surely, he isn't ready to propose. I undo the bow and start to unwrap it.

"Most guys in high school give their girlfriends their class rings to wear, and I never gave you mine." I breathe a little easier, thinking that it's just his class ring in the box. I've got it unwrapped, but he puts his hand on top of mine to stop me from opening it. "My mom said sometimes girls wear promise rings. Like a pre-engagement ring." He takes his hand away. "That's what this is."

Inside the box is this beautiful silver ring with two tiny diamonds mounted so they wrap around each other. Nothing but love shines from Cal's eyes, and my heart swells up.

He does love me. He isn't just saying the words. He really wants to spend the rest of his life with me. This gift is practically a proposal. It's the commitment that I never thought he'd make, that I wasn't sure if he loved me enough to make. All the doubts and the second-guessing burn away in the brilliance of those two little diamonds.

I slip the ring on and admire it on my hand. It fits perfectly. "It's beautiful." I put my arms around his neck and kiss him. I feel like all the broken pieces of my dreams fall back together during that kiss. Like it's going to all work out all right. I can go to college with Cal. I can major in Education, be on the dance team, find a studio in Knoxville. There will be plenty of opportunities to dance in different ensembles. As long as we get to be together, that's what's important. That's the only big picture thing I should worry about.

Even God's in agreement because He gave me the sign. Celeste is a professional. She knows what she's talking about. I'll never be in the company. I need to put my focus on my relationship with Cal.

Our kisses become more passionate and suddenly I can't remember why I've been waiting. I love him and he loves me. He's committed to loving me. This ring *proves* that he really wants to marry me. Waiting for marriage doesn't seem necessary when we are making the commitment now. Sophie was right. It's about love and commitment.

I need him. I need to physically feel his love for me. I've never needed anything so much as this right now. This is the way he can take care of me. Tears sting my eyes, but I blink them back.

Things start to heat up, but I don't stop him. This is what it means to love someone. To give them everything. To commit one hundred percent.

Somehow it doesn't feel like a commitment, though. It feels like he's saving me from falling to pieces. I don't think I can face tomorrow without this.

"Cal, do you promise me forever?"

"Yes. Forever. I love you, Madison."

"Then I'm ready."

"Are you sure?" he asks. I nod, and he kisses me.

He pulls a condom out of his wallet and sets it on my bedside table then knocks the decorative pillows and my stuffed animals off the bed.

Jacob the dog and Edward the lion are staring at me from the floor as if to remind me of choices and growing up.

Quit staring, boys. I need this.

Calvin is gentle and loving every step of the way. He makes me feel beautiful and delicate instead of like the freakishly large Amazon I am.

Afterward, we get under the covers, and he wraps me in his arms and promptly falls asleep. I'm happy, because I know it made him happy, but a little disappointed and honestly, still wanting more. Maybe I'll have the courage to tell him what I need next time. We've got the rest of our lives to work it out.

I slip out of bed, get dressed, and go to the bathroom. I thought I would feel different. I thought it would heal my broken heart, but instead I just feel this deep, overwhelming emptiness. I slide to the floor and start sobbing. In trading one dream for another, did I just make the biggest mistake of my life?

My virginity is gone. I *woo'd in haste and mean to wed at leisure.* Even Shakespeare thinks I should have waited. *A bliss in proof, and proved, a very woe. What's done is done.* I chose Calvin. It's a relief, really.

I pull myself together and splash my face with cool water, then wake Cal with a kiss. "You have to go home. If our neighbors see your car in the driveway in the morning, they'll tell my parents."

A little of his normal confident attitude comes back. "While the cat's away..." He pulls me back into the bed and under the covers. His lips graze my neck. He slips his hands under my sweatshirt and pulls me tight against him. "Mmm, you smell good. You are amazing."

I lay my head on his chest and listen to his heartbeat, so true, in rhythm with mine, forever. Linked forever. Right or wrong, I made my choice.

I would like nothing better than to listen to his heart all night long, stay wrapped in his arms, so safe and warm and comforting. Where I belong now.

But I force myself to pull away. "I'm serious. You have to go."

He sighs. "All right." His lips brush mine, before his warmth is stripped from me. He gathers his clothes, and I watch him dress. I giggle when he dives back on the bed for more kissing. I nibble his earlobe and kiss his neck while he puts on his shoes. He pulls me out of the bed for one more hug and kiss before he puts on his coat, digs out his keys, and goes to the door.

"See you tomorrow, lover girl.

> *A sign*
>   *Can't make it out*
> *But I know it's for me*
>   *It sets me free*
> *To do the thing*
>   *No one says I shouldn't*
> *Except you.*
>   *A voice in my head*
> *I thought you were dead*
>   *Now I see*
>   *It says, "Vacancy."*

That emptiness inside is screaming in my head.

"Shut up already!"

I crumple the scrap of paper with the scrawled poem. This time, instead of shoving it in the box, I jerk the box out from under my bed and run out to the garage. *What's done is done.* I get an old metal bucket and dump the stupid, sappy, meaningless words into it. Then I drop a match in and watch it all burn.

Chapter Nineteen

I get the official word from Ms. Turpin that I didn't get the scholarship before the next performance. I expected it, but it still hurts. I sit at the dressing table, trying to get my little maid hat secured, trying not to cry. Megan comes and stands next to me, looking at me in the mirror. She sighs. I still want to hate her. I still can't. She looks like a porcelain doll with her perfect dancer-sized body and her stage makeup on.

"I'm sorry," she says.

"Why are you sorry? You're the better dancer. You deserve it."

"Do I?"

"What do you mean? Of course, you do."

"I thought your audition was better than mine. Especially your jazz piece. I think they just gave me the scholarship because they felt sorry for me."

My face crinkles up, and I turn to her. "Why?"

"My dad was a firefighter. He was killed in a fire a few months ago."

"Oh. I'm so sorry." I can't even imagine losing my dad.

"Yeah. It's been rough." She looks at her feet. "Everyone's been so nice. Sometimes, too nice, you know?" She looks back at me. "It's a lot. Like this. I'm not sure if I got this part because I deserved it, or they wanted me to have it to give me something to focus on. And I'm not sure I got the scholarship because I earned it, or because … you know, pity."

My mouth goes dry. I don't want her to think I pity her either, so I put on a smile and speak truth to her doubt. "Well, I think you're an amazing dancer, and you definitely earned both. Congratulations on the scholarship."

"Thanks. What will you do? Will you still take classes?"

My chest gets heavy. I busy myself cleaning up the dressing table. "I don't think so. I guess it just wasn't meant to be." I chose Cal. And that's okay.

"I'm sorry to hear that. I think you're an amazing dancer too. Plus, I was hoping we'd have some classes together, so we could get to be friends."

"I guess we'll have to find another way to do that."

She smiles. "I'd like that."

The next few days—when I'm not thinking about the company— are pure bliss. If I'm not at the theatre or the Pansy, I'm with Cal. There's a closeness between us, an intimacy, that thrills me. Every time he looks at me, I remember the feeling of his arms around me, and I get all tingly inside. I think about how that is the place I belong. Forever. I write love poems every day, even though Cal laughs at them and teases me for being a hopeless romantic.

> *I haven't felt warm since I lay in your arms*
> *or felt your lips parting kiss,*
> *If I asked, would you stay with me all through my life*
> *So I can keep feeling like this?*

I beg Cal to go caroling with me and the youth group Saturday night. He only agrees because I have a performance that afternoon and another one Sunday night, and I won't be able to see him again until Monday. But I regret inviting him. We go in the church van, and I have to introduce him around. Kendra and Kevin are there looking adorable in Santa hats and holding hands.

Cal snickers when he sees the hats. "Can we leave right away and not stay for the hot chocolate and cookies? I'm sure I'll be over my sweetness quota by then."

I nudge him with my elbow and hope no one heard.

At the first nursing home, Paul reminds us that many of the patients are lonely and crave any kind of contact. Holding their hands, sitting beside them, or giving them a hug will mean a lot to them.

Cal whispers this time. "I'm here, but I'm not touching any old people."

He stands off to the side and doesn't even sing as the rest of us walk around the common room and try to interact with the residents. Most of them have big grins. A lot of them sing along. We sing four carols and then stay another fifteen minutes. Cal sneaks out and waits by the van.

He makes more snide comments as we drive. At the next place, he refuses to go in anymore. We go to Parker House last, where Nathan works. I see him with his family visiting his grandparents as we pass the dining room. When they hear us singing, they bring his grandparents into the common room. He smiles at me. I don't know why, but it makes me feel sick. Sick to my stomach and sick at heart. I'm sure that if I don't leave, I'll throw up all over the bald man in the wheelchair that I'm standing next to.

Kendra follows me to the bathroom. "What's wrong? Are you sick?"

I stand over the sink, willing myself to breathe. I shake my head, then nod.

She pulls out a paper towel and wets it. "Here. Put this on the back of your neck. You're white as a sheet."

"I'm sorry about the way Cal's acting. I never should have..." My eyes tear up. "I always think he'll be... Is it wrong for me to want him to be different? When you love someone, you're supposed to love all of him, right? You're not supposed to want to change him. I mean, so what if old people freak him out? I shouldn't have pushed him to come."

She sighs. "Have you heard about Charlie?"

I'm confused by the abrupt change of subject. Charlie's her older brother. "No. Is something wrong?" I'm wracking my brain to remember if I've seen his name under prayer requests.

"He's in rehab. He's a drug addict."

My eyes go wide. "Charlie? No way."

"Yeah. The thing is, we all denied it for at least a year. He always apologized after, when he did stupid or mean stuff when he was high. We blamed his friends. We blamed the drugs. We just couldn't bring ourselves to blame him. We love him. We wanted to believe that he was the same person he'd always been. But that was wrong of us. Drugs change people. And sometimes when you refuse to see that you can't change them back, you're not being honest with yourself. In Charlie's case, we enabled him."

I frown at her and try to hear what she's really saying. "You think I'm trying to make Cal into something he's not?"

"No. I'm saying maybe you're lying to yourself about who he really is. It's easy to do when you love someone."

Jen Statler, another friend from youth group, comes in and tells us that it's time to go. "Um, Nathan's out there. He's worried about you."

Nathan. I'd hoped he'd left. Why does he have to be so freaking perfect? It's so hard not to compare him to Cal. *Of course*, Cal can't measure up to him. I put on a smile and follow them out of the bathroom.

Nathan is leaning against the wall, but he stands up when we come out. "Hey. Are you okay?"

"I'm good. I just, um, had some girl problems." *Well, boy problems anyway.*

His face gets red. "You looked sick."

"Sometimes cramps can make me nauseated." That is not a lie.

"Oh, sorry." He runs a hand through his hair. "We're leaving for Atlanta tonight. We'll be there all week. So, I'll see you when we get back."

"Okay. I'm not working much this week anyway. *Nutcracker.*"

"Yeah, well, break a leg."

"Thanks."

When I turn to leave Cal is standing at the end of the hall giving me a murderous glare. "Kendra said you weren't feeling well, and I come find you flirting with that dude from the Pansy."

"I don't feel well. And we were just talking. I wasn't flirting." I roll my eyes and brush past him. "Come on, they're waiting on us."

Cal texts Joey on the way back to the church, and he's waiting when we arrive.

"I thought you were coming to my house," I say.

He grunts and looks disgusted. "After that? I need a drink." He bolts so fast when we get out of the van it's like he's afraid we're contagious.

Every time Kendra's words try to creep into my thoughts that night, I shove them aside. Cal's not an addict. It's not the same thing.

Chapter Twenty

$\mathcal{I}$m concerned about my sister dropping by, which she has done a couple of times already, or my neighbors reporting Cal's car in the driveway to my parents, so I don't let him come over much. He's anxious to make love again, but I put him off. I don't know why. On the one hand, I can't wait to feel that closeness again, but I keep having these nagging feelings that I did it for all the wrong reasons. I try to explain to Cal how heartbroken I was that night over Celeste's comments, but he doesn't get why that matters. He can't understand why I'm stalling. And I can't explain about the emptiness I felt afterwards.

I did it, though. And to me, it means that I've committed to him for life. So I try to focus on that and how relieved I am to have a specific plan mapped out that doesn't depend on taking classes I can't afford and the May auditions for Company Two. I slack off on my barre work.

We mostly hang out at his mom's house when I'm not at performances. He plays this intense computer game called *Battlegrounds*, or something. Sometimes, I read. I'm just content to be together. His sister is there most of the time, and there is no way I'm making out with him again when she's around.

I'm glad Nathan is still on vacation with his family. I don't have to tell him that I've decided to go to UT and be on the dance team. Seeing his disappointment in me would spoil everything.

Cal and I go shopping together with the money my mom left me to buy a new comforter. It's part of my Christmas present. My current one is frilly white with pink ribbons on it. Very little girl. I'm so excited about picking out a new one with Cal. Like we're already married.

"I want it to match my room, but I want it to be kind of neutral too."

"Why don't I go in the electronics store while you shop."

There would have to be an electronics store right next door. "I wanted you to help me pick." He doesn't see how disappointed I am. "What if this is the comforter that we have on our bed in our first house? Don't you want some say in what it looks like?"

"Not really." I frown. "Did you never notice the Spartan style I got going on in my room? I don't care about comforters and curtains."

"But it will be ours. Both of ours. Someday."

He laughs and kisses the tip my nose. "This little game of house you're playing is cute, but I'm going next door. I'm sure whatever you pick will be perfect." He walks away, then turns and adds, "For both of us."

I choose a gray-blue with a geometric design. The colors in it are in my carpet and my curtains, but they aren't girly at all. I think he'll like it. I picture it in our future bedroom with some accent pillows. It *will* be perfect.

My parents are in the audience on the twenty-first. I'm only in one more show, a matinee on the twenty-third, so it's my last nighttime performance. I like the night shows better, and my heart is heavy. Who knows when I'll get to dance in a big show like this again? Will I even perform *en pointe* again? After curtain call, I look for my parents, but instead I find Nathan and his sister, Caroline.

She's bouncing up and down on the balls of her feet. "You were amazing," she says and hands me a bouquet of pink roses.

"Wow. Thank you." I glance at Nathan and thank him too.

"My mom couldn't bring her, so I volunteered," he explains.

"I bet she was shocked." I laugh when he nods. "Did you see my parents anywhere?" I ask, but they didn't. I ask Caroline who her favorite was in the company, so I can get her some autographed shoes, and she says me. I laugh, but really, it hurts so much. My eyes prickle as I blink back tears, because I know I'll never be anyone's favorite in the company. I'll never autograph *my* pointe shoes. I have to work really hard to keep the smile on my face. "I'm not in the company. Why don't I just pick someone for you?"

I ask them to wait and come back with a pair of Monica's shoes. "She was the Sugar Plum fairy," I tell her, and she beams. I avoid Nathan's eyes as I talk to Caroline about the show, but eventually I look up at him.

He's frowning. "What's wrong?" he asks.

I smile. "Nothing. Everything's…perfect. Thanks for coming."

"I thought you were great," he said. "But I fell asleep during the second half," he admits.

I nod. "It's a very long half for a non-dancer. I'm glad you came tonight. It's my last night." The words are hard to get out. My last night. My last nighttime performance with City Ballet. I press my lips together and take a deep breath.

Nathan frowns again. Darn him. How can he be so perceptive? He's a *guy* for crying out loud.

"You working tomorrow?" he asks.

I don't trust my voice, so I nod. Caroline gives me a hug. "Thanks for these," she says, and I nod again, the same fake smile plastered on my face. Nathan pulls her away, and they say goodbye. I just give them a little wave then turn and run to the dressing rooms.

I find a text from my mom saying that my dad's back was bothering him, so they left at intermission. When I get home, they're already in bed, but there's a note saying how much they enjoyed the show, and what a great job I did and flowers in a vase on my dresser.

I do a pretty good job of avoiding Nathan, since it's Friday and we're busy. We close in an hour, so I'm trying to get things cleaned up, hoping no new customers will come in. I hear the bell on the door and look up anxiously. It's Calvin, wearing new clothes and a forties style hat, which he tips at me as he walks by the counter with a grin and a wink. I shake my head. We have different ideas about what constitutes good fashion, but I give him points for his boldness.

Nathan comes up behind me as I watch Cal walk into the dining room. "What do you see in him?" he asks.

I smile. "I love him."

His lip curls up in a disgusted snarl. "Name five things you love about him," he challenges.

Why does he have to question everything? Is he so intent on throwing me off balance? But this should be easy. Only five things.

"I love that he's so smart." Except for when he's being condescending, which happens more and more often since he started college.

"That's one," Nathan says.

"Um," I hesitate. Why is this so hard? "I love his eyes." Now more than ever his eyes set me on fire.

"Physical things don't count."

"Why not?"

"That's lust, not love. I want you to name character traits."

I sigh and wipe the counter, thinking. "I love that he acts like a gentlemen and opens doors for me and—"

"Never pressures you to have sex. Never lies about you to his friends." His voice drips with sarcasm. "Such a gentlemen."

My lips tighten into a thin line. "I don't have to justify how I feel to you."

"If you can't name five things that you love about that dipstick, then you couldn't possibly be in love with him."

"Can you name five things you love about Candace right off the top of your head?"

"No." He looks down at the floor. "That's why I broke up with her."

"Oh. I'm sorry." I put my hand on his arm.

He shrugs my hand off and steps back. "Don't be. She wasn't the one."

"Well, Calvin is the one." He has to be. I made my choice. I twirl the promise ring around my finger.

Nathan sees the ring for the first time. "That's not an engagement ring, is it?"

"It's a promise ring."

"What did he promise you?"

"I promised him that I would say yes when he does ask me to marry him."

He grunts and mumbles something under his breath, but the only word I catch is *pants*. "You want to spend the rest of your life with him when you can't even name five things that you love about him?"

"I can. I just need some time to think about it."

He raises his eyebrows. "Maddy, it's so obvious that you're not really in love with him. He's a jerk. He treats you like crap, and you just take it because you've got this stupid guilt complex."

"He doesn't treat me like crap. He loves me. And there are tons of things I love about him. Just give me a minute." But I honestly can't come up with anything else that I love about him that isn't physical. All I can remember is his snarkiness and teasing. And the fact that, until he gave me this ring, I was questioning whether he loved me at all.

It can't be true.

I know it's not true. I love Calvin. I love the way he looks at me. It makes me feel all tingly inside. I love… I love his voice in my ear, the way he kisses me, the way he made love to me, and how it made me feel desirable, special. *Is that really just lust?*

I lose the use of my knees. I lean against the counter for support. It can't be true.

Can it?

I see Nathan look around to make sure Abdulla is still in his office before he tugs me into the kitchen where we can't be seen. Sandy is here unloading the dishwasher. Steve is here too, making tomorrow's dough.

Sandy looks at me. "What's wrong?"

I look helplessly at Nathan. "Would you cover the counter for a minute?" he asks her.

She carries a stack of plates to put away under the counter.

"I'm sorry. I didn't mean to upset you," Nathan says. "I just thought…"

"What?" Now I'm mad. I'm really mad at myself, but I take it out on him. "You just thought you'd turn my whole life upside down? Well, it won't work, because it's not true. It's not just a guilt complex. That's ridiculous." I push him. He doesn't budge from my push, but he steps back. I want to slap him. I raise my hand to do it, but he easily catches my arm. Everything starts to look blurry.

"Don't kill the messenger." His crinkled brow softens. "Look, if it's not true, then good. I'm glad." He walks over to the sink and picks up another stack of clean plates. My hands ball up into fists. He stops in front of me. "Just think about it, before you do something you'll regret."

A tear slips out of my eye. "It's too late," I whisper. His face falls. He knows what I'm saying. He closes his eyes and sighs. When he opens his eyes there's anger there. I look down at my hands, my feet, anywhere but into his accusing eyes. He walks away, leaving me feeling humiliated.

Chapter Twenty-one

*W*hen my shift ends, I go in the dining room and find Calvin and some of his friends from high school being asked to leave by Abdulla. I feel like my body is made of lead; every movement is an effort. I look to Calvin expecting him to notice, to say something, to fix this, to prove Nathan wrong.

"Hey baby." He puts an arm around me as we walk to the door. "I'm going to head over to Joey's to play poker."

I just nod. *Notice.* "I thought you came to see me," I say when we get to his car.

"I did see you." He kisses me then gets in. "But you have curfew in an hour, little girl, remember?"

I guess it's selfish to expect him to want to spend that hour with me. He kisses me once more and then leaves. I can't go home. I feel like I'm in shock or something. There's no one else in the parking lot, so I slip around to the back and climb up to the roof.

It looks like the last people up here had quite a party. There are empty beer bottles and other pieces of trash scattered around. The chairs are wet with frost. It's probably forty degrees, but I'm numb. I don't feel it. I lie on my back and dangle my feet off the edge and stare up at the sky. It's cloudy. All that's up there is inky black nothing. No stars. *Figures.*

I'm sure I can come up with four more things that I love about Calvin that aren't physical. There's a lot more to him than his intelligence and my physical attraction to him. There has to be. I'm committed to him.

Or did I commit to him by default? Did I settle? Did I grab on to him because my dreams were falling apart around me? Did I forgive him over and over because of what happened with

Nathan? My breathing becomes hard and fast, like there's a weight on my chest.

I try to approach it from another angle. What qualities do I want in a husband? Honesty, a strong work ethic, Godly values, loves children and family, supports my dreams, someone who really sees me and gets me.

I feel sick. I sit up and pull my knees to my chest.

The tears start dripping out of my eyes in a never-ending stream. There's no point trying to wipe them away. *O Cunning Love! With tears thou keep'st me blind, Lest eyes well-seeing thy foul faults should find.*

Could I have picked someone more opposite from my ideal? How did I let this happen? *The heart is deceitful above all things.*

"I thought You gave me a sign." God knows my heart but saying it out loud might help me come to terms with it. "I thought You were telling me that Calvin is the one. Did I make the wrong choice—again? I just wanted to do what You wanted me to do, but I blew it. I *yoked* myself to a non-believer. Could You have been more clear? It's right there in the Bible. And I just ignored it completely. I just wanted—I *needed*—to feel his love for me." Then it hits me. I wanted to *feel* his love for me because he wasn't *showing* me love. "Oh, God, I'm so sorry. There's no workaround for sin. I let You down." I'm sobbing now, and my stomach aches. How could I make such a mess of things?

I stare at the streetlight on the other side of the parking lot until it's all I can see. Until it's all there is. Because my brain can't process the very idea that I don't really love Calvin, that I'm going to spend the rest of my life with a guy who's not *The One*."

There must be a way for me to fix this. To make it right.

I don't know how much time passes. My mom's probably wondering where I am. I should call, but I just sit there. I hear cars leaving the parking lot. The closers have left.

I hear footsteps. Still, I don't move.

Nathan.

He sits beside me.

I pull a tissue from my pocket and wipe my eyes and blow my nose. "I didn't do what you said," I say. "I didn't have any objectivity.

I was so upset because of what Celeste said… I thought it was a sign. I just needed… I just wanted…" My dripping tears turn back into sobs. He lets me cry and pats my back.

"Who's Celeste?"

I only had the one tissue, so I swipe at my face with the back of my gloved hand and sniff. "She's one of the best dancers in the company. She practically called me a freak of nature."

"What? Why?"

"She said I was too tall and broad-shouldered, and my feet were huge. She said I'd never be in the company because of my body type, not to mention my poor turnout and extension. She's right, too. That's why they gave me that solo part, because I didn't fit in with the other dancers."

"But I think you're missing the point. They gave you a solo part. They believed you were good enough to be in the show, so they made a part for you. Not every dancer has the same body type, that's stupid."

"Yes, they do. Company directors only choose certain types, so they'll all look alike. I don't have a chance of being in the company, no matter how hard I work."

"I don't believe that. And you shouldn't either. You should still try out if that's your dream."

I bury my face in my knees. "It doesn't matter. It's too late. I made my choice." And I've got to stick with my commitment, so God can forgive me. God hates divorce. I made a commitment to Cal. I can't compound my sin by walking away from that.

He pulls on my ponytail. "I can't hear you."

I turn my face towards him. "I said it doesn't matter. It's too late now."

"I don't understand. The tryouts are in May, right?"

I pull the hood up on my coat and tuck my hands under my arms. "I mean, I chose Calvin. I chose a life with him. He doesn't want me to be in the company. He wants me to come to UT. And now I'm committed to him."

"Not unless that's a wedding ring."

"It might as well be. I put on the ring. I had sex with him." Nathan winces at that. "I didn't look at him objectively. I didn't choose well.

But I made my choice, so I'm just going to have to be happy with it."

"I get what you're saying, but you're seventeen. Cut yourself some slack. You're allowed to make mistakes. If you're not really in love with him, you need to end it."

"But it will totally break his heart." And God's.

"Big freaking deal. You can't give up your dreams just because you don't want to break his heart. He's a big boy. He'll get over it." He looks over at the empty parking lot. "I did."

I close my eyes to push away the memory of Nathan's face when he yelled at me and broke up with me in front of everyone. I hate that I hurt him. I hate it with everything I am. I can't bear the thought of doing that to Calvin.

"I think I have to try to keep my commitment. I have to see if he's worth giving up my dreams for. This whole week I've been so relieved that I didn't have to worry about it anymore. No company. No killing myself to get ready for auditions. No dance classes. No difficult conversation with my parents." I bang my head against my knees a few times, push my hood off, and wipe my eyes again. "Teaching school and maybe coaching a dance team—that's a good dream too." I can be happy with that.

He reaches up and tucks a hair that's come out of my ponytail behind my ear. "Ballerina girl, you have to dance. It will break your heart if you don't. I saw your face when you said it was your last night."

"How do you know me so well? Why do you even care?" My phone buzzes in my pocket with a text from my mom. I text back that I'm on my way. "I have to go."

"Good. It's freezing up here." He stands and offers his hand to pull me up. "Next time you want to talk, can we do it inside?" he asks as we climb down the ladder.

"I came up here to be alone. Nobody asked you to freeze with me."

He waits until we're walking side by side. "Friends don't let friends freeze alone," he says.

I smile and nudge him with my elbow. "You're a goober, you know that?"

He nudges me back. "But I'm a studly goober, so that makes it all right."

I invite Cal to the Christmas Eve service at our church, but he refuses. It's such a beautiful candlelight service that I think maybe it could touch his heart or at least get him thinking about God in ways that I've never been able to. If he becomes a believer, then everything will change. Everything will be okay. I beg and plead until he gives in, but only because I said he would score points with my parents for going. I watch him throughout the service and realize that his head is not in the right place to really hear what's being said. When it comes to the part where we do a corporate confession of sin, I feel like a big hypocrite. I have to run to the bathroom, so I don't melt down in front of everyone.

Afterward, we have our traditional big family dinner and exchange gifts. My dad doesn't even offer us any wine this time. I elbow Cal in the ribs before he has a chance to ask for a beer. He opens the fancy gaming headset I got him and is ready to leave after that, so he can go try it out. I'm glad he likes it. He dropped plenty of hints, so I made sure his mom wasn't getting it. She coordinated with me to take over his phone plan instead and is going to take him to pick out a better phone and upgrade the plan.

We go to his mom's apartment on Christmas Day. Lyla is there. She and Cal give their mom a kitten and all the accessories. I think kittens are adorable for about five seconds, and then they lick you with that sandpaper tongue, and it's all over. That gives me chills. I got ringworm from a neighbor's cat when I was little and have never liked them since. I'm a dog person. How did I not know that Cal is a cat person? I thought we had so much in common.

I sit next to Lyla on the couch and show her the ring Cal gave me and thank her.

"For what?" she asks.

"Cal said that you loaned him the money. I thought you probably helped him pick it out too."

She looks at me funny. "You must have misunderstood. I didn't loan him the money."

Cal and his mom are busy playing with the kitten and don't

hear us. I'm sure I didn't misunderstand. He lied to me. But why?

I try to cover my surprise and hurt with a smile. "Huh. I guess I got it wrong." I redirect by laughing at the kitten. He *is* cute. Just keep that tongue away from me. *Ick!*

"Would you grab me a soda?" Cal asks me from the floor.

"Sure."

I work dayshift the week after Christmas and go out with Calvin every night. I feel like an observer, like I'm not really there. I make sure we don't get into a situation where we're alone because I know what he wants to do, and I feel like I just met him.

Who is this guy?

Everyone was right. He treats me like crap. Well, it's more like he's indifferent. I wait on him hand and foot. I compliment him and never miss an opportunity to give his ego a little boost. And he never reciprocates. Now even his "I love yous" feel like a part he's playing to keep me happy, so I'll keep giving him what he wants. Maybe he doesn't really know what true love looks like. His parents didn't give him a great example. Our relationship is very surface level.

Who is this guy?

And who am I?

I don't even recognize this person that is Calvin's girlfriend. We go where he wants to go. Eat what he wants to eat. I don't even like Chinese food! I pay for most of it—I used to pay for it all. We usually take my car, so I'm paying for the gas too, and I'm totally okay with it because I know it makes him happy. I'm like this lovesick puppy. No wonder he loves me. It's hard not to love the perfect girlfriend that adores you. But now that I'm watching, I don't adore him. I'm not even sure I like him.

What have I done?

That stupid pamphlet about unhealthy relationships keeps flashing before my eyes. Yes, we isolate ourselves from others. Yes, my friends say I act differently. Now I see why. Yes, I'm keeping secrets as well as telling lies. I can answer yes to three out of the four questions. And when I read them the first time, I didn't even see it. How pathetic is that? Kendra was right. I've been lying to myself about who Cal is. I somehow built him up in my mind as somebody else. I'm in love with a made-up version of him, not the real Cal.

We babysit for Kaitlyn the last night that he's going to be in town. They've been going on weekly date nights to help them get their relationship back on track. It seems to be working. No more fighting. And they look at each other again with that same love I see in my parents' eyes. Kayleigh's going to start back to nursing school in the summer, so Mom and I can watch Kaitlyn. She told me he finally confessed it was an ego thing. He wanted to be able to solely provide for his family, so she could stay at home. He didn't mean to squash her dreams in the process.

I cuddle Kaitlyn to me and kiss her head. She smells so good.

Calvin narrows his eyes at me, a look of disgust on his face. He has to drive to St. Louis to meet his mom tomorrow because there is a family reunion there on New Year's Day. I start back to school next Monday, so he'll go straight back to Knoxville from there even though he has a few more days before he starts classes.

My heart keeps insisting that I'm just being overcritical. None of this stuff bothered me before. He loves me in the way he knows how. That will grow over time. That's what's important, right? Nathan's stupid list is just that. But as I step back and watch him treat Kaitlyn like she's an alien instead of an adorable toddler, I want to cry.

"This isn't how I wanted to spend our last night together," he says for the third time.

I'm rocking Kaitlyn to sleep, and he's sprawled out in the floor watching TV. It's ten thirty and my sister and Derrick are due home soon.

"I thought she'd go down way before this," I whisper over her head. It's a lie. One of many I've told this week. I feel terrible, but I would feel worse if we made love again.

Wouldn't I?

I'm so confused.

I take Kaitlyn to her room and finally put her down. When I come back to the living room Calvin pulls me to the couch and starts kissing me. I'm so torn because I really want to. He's pushing all the right buttons.

"We can't," I manage to say. "They'll be home any minute."

He sits back and crosses his arms on his chest. "Fine."

Okay. This is it. The ultimate test. If he really loves me and gets me this will prove it. I snuggle up to him, putting my head on his chest. I can't bear to look into his eyes.

"What would you say if I told you that I don't want to go to UT?" The words come out thickly, like I've got peanut butter on the roof of my mouth.

"Why not?" He's already mad at me, and his response is stiff and sharp.

I swallow. "I want to take classes and try out in May for the City Ballet Company."

"You don't want to go to college at all?" He makes a kind of half-laugh, half-snort noise.

I tell him about how I could go to Bellmeade. "I want to dance with the company while I earn a degree and then open my own studio."

His body is shaking with laughter now. "You're kidding, right? Those are just pipe dreams. You can't make a living like that. That's just crazy. You barely got that little part in the *Nutcracker*. What makes you think you're good enough to be in their ballet company or teach? That dancer even said you wouldn't make it."

I have to work very hard to keep my voice even. There are tears pooling in my eyes, and my throat feels like it's closing up. "I can make a decent income from teaching dance. And then later, I can sell out and just teach part-time, so I can have kids and be a stay-at-home mom."

This is my dream. Support it. Please. Please. Please. I can overlook anything else.

The tears are rolling down my face now, wetting his shirt.

"Your parents will freak if you tell them this little fantasy of yours." He pauses. And I pray he's just adjusting to the idea. "They have a dance team at UT, you know." Another pause and a sigh. "And how many kids are we talking about?"

"Dance teams don't have ballet companies. It's not the same. Don't you want to have kids?" Another thing we've never discussed.

"Not really. They kind of take over your life."

"They enrich your life," I manage to sputter out.

"If you say so." I think he finally notices that I'm upset because he adds, "one or two might be all right," as if this is some great consolation on his part.

I hear the garage door open and pretend that I have to go to the bathroom. When I come back out to greet Kayleigh and Derrick, I've got a mask firmly in place.

All the way back to my house, I hide my tears. There's a lot of tension in the air. I've made him mad, I think. He stays focused on the music playing and driving instead of trying to talk. It's one more strike against him that I'm crying next to him, and he's completely oblivious. What kind of boyfriend doesn't notice? A voice in the back of my head says, *"Maybe he does notice and just doesn't care because he's mad."*

It's still thirty minutes before my curfew when we pull into the driveway, and I know he wants to make out, but it is not happening. I want to break up with him right now. I want to give him back his ring and explain that I've made a mistake, but I can't. If I do it now, he'll blow off his trip. And I need to be away from him to clear my head.

"I've got a terrible headache," I lie—again. "Have a safe trip tomorrow." I lean over and kiss him goodbye and start to get out of the car, but he grabs my arm.

"We're not going to see each other for a long time and that's all I get? A peck?" He pulls me into a deeper kiss, but when his hands get involved, I push him away. "Are we ever going to do it again?" he asks. "You said you liked it. Did I do something wrong?"

My resolve softens a little at that. I kiss him again. Remembering. Which is not smart. "No," I say, and let him touch me this time. "It's just… I told you, I don't feel good." My thinking is fuzzy. His arms are warm and strong and my place inside them feels right. I'm having trouble remembering that I'm hurt and disappointed.

"Well. You don't feel well."

He blows it with that. Is it really the time to be correcting my grammar? I pull away, angry now. "Whatever." I get out of the car. "Call me when you get to St. Louis."

I go inside and cry myself to sleep and wake up the next morning with the terrible headache I supposedly had last night. Payback for my lies.

Chapter Twenty-two

*I*ve been sullen and moody at work, and Nathan has given me a lot of space. Which is good, but weird. I need space. I have a huge decision to make. But he's such a great listener and gives such good advice that I want to tell him what I'm feeling. I don't understand why I can talk to him so easily, but not to Cal. It would be wrong to lay all this on Nathan, though, and his advice is biased anyway since he hates Cal.

Instead of calls, Cal and I get into a habit of texting back and forth at bedtime. Which is so much easier as I try to figure out what to do. His eyes are my downfall. I've only got three more weekdays of winter break and a weekend. I have to tell him how I'm feeling, but my cowardice is paralyzing. *Thus conscience does make cowards of us all.*

Tonight, I'm determined. I go first so there's no lovey-dovey stuff from him to sidetrack me.

Me:

> *I'm very unhappy.*

I wait about fifteen minutes before he replies. He's probably playing online games. That's what he does all day when I'm at work.

Cal:

> *What's up?*
> *I think we made a mistake. I shouldn't have accepted your promise ring before we talked about our future.*
>> *Please don't say that. We love each other.*
>> *The future will take care of itself.*
> *That's what I used to think, but now I'm not sure.*
>> *Why?*

We don't want the same things. I'm scared. I don't want to end up divorced.
I want whatever makes you happy.
I don't think you know what that is.

The cursor blinks twenty-three times before I hit send. I wait for a few minutes, and then he calls.

"How can you say that?" he asks before I even say hello. "I love you. You mean everything to me. You're all I have. I can't lose you, Madison. I can't."

I don't know what I'm supposed to say to that. "I am not all you have."

"All that matters." There's a pause. "I didn't want to tell you, but I'm on probation for my scholarship. If I don't pull my grades up this semester, I'll lose it."

"So you kept it from me. And you lied about how you got the money for the ring. Can I even trust you anymore?"

"Yes, you can. I tell you important stuff. I just didn't want you to get upset about my grades. I didn't want it to spoil Christmas. And I cashed in some bonds to buy the ring. They weren't fully mature, and I knew you'd feel guilty if you knew I'd spent them on you."

This is true. I feel super guilty knowing he did that. Especially since I don't want it anymore.

"What about how you hardly ever call me and rarely respond to my texts? What's your excuse for that? I pour out my heart to you, thinking we're on the same page about stuff, and you don't even know what page I'm on."

"Speaking of pages, dang Madison, those text threads are practically longer than my reading assignments for literature. You can't really expect me to read them all. College life is busy."

"Because God forbid you should miss fifteen minutes of game time."

He's quiet for a minute or so. "Look, you're just taking a few little things I did and blowing them out of proportion, like you always do. Why don't we talk about this tomorrow after you've cooled off? Okay?"

"I don't think there's anything else to say. I want to break up."

"You're just mad right now. That's all. You don't mean that."

"I'm sorry, Cal. I really am, but I do mean it."

I disconnect. My heart bursts with the burden of how I'm hurting him.

That deep, horrible, empty feeling is back. All this time, I've been thinking that because of him my life was complete. I couldn't wait for our future together to start. But it was all a lie—to him, to myself. A future with him is not what I want at all. He is not the one. And even if he was, it's my relationship with God that should fill me up—not my relationship with any person.

I've neglected God as I've tried to be the perfect girlfriend. How messed up is that? And now I've disappointed God so completely that I'm not sure He can forgive me.

My phone rings again, but I turn it off.

The worst part is, I can't tell him why. I can't say, "You don't support my dreams," because he'll say anything right now to keep me from breaking up with him. He'll pretend to be something he's not. He might even agree to go to church with me just to prove that he's willing to do anything for us. But that's not who he is. And he should have someone who loves him for who he is.

Nathan's right. I'm not in love with Cal. I was in love with being in love, with having a relationship, with having someone tell me that he loved me, with the physical stuff. I do care about him.

But it's not the forever kind of love that I want.

The pain of it puts the poetry in my head.

A Shakespearean sonnet:

> *I thought for you I would, I could give all*
> *Abandon home, forsake friend's pleas, for you*
> *My own self lost inside your need, your call*
> *Forget my dreams, let yours become mine too.*
>
> *When all myself is given to your heart*
> *Where then do I begin and do I end?*
> *I'm lost, undone each time we have to part.*
> *Alone, I look for myself in the wind.*

But I am gone. I have become your cup.
Empty, poured out so you will not have need.
Shouldn't your love, your passion fill me up?
Will I run dry one day? Fear plants its seed.

If you gave back one part of your own soul
I would, I could have stayed and been made whole.

I text it to Cal the next morning. I preface it with an apology. I tell him that he will always have a piece of my heart, but that I can't marry him. And that I can't really love him when I don't trust him, and when our plans for the future are so different.

Three hours after I send the text, he calls. I have to go to work soon. I know it's him without even looking. I can feel his pain through the phone, and I start to cry.

"I don't think I can talk about this now," I say as I answer, my voice soft and shaky.

"Well, we're going to talk about it!" he yells. "Are you out of your freaking mind? You can't break up with me with a stupid poem in a text. You can't break up with me at all. You said this was forever. You're the one who made me a promise. You took the ring." A stream of curse words follows. "Why are you doing this?"

I drag in a stilted breath. "I broke up with you on the phone yesterday. The text was just to make sure you understood. It's all in the poem."

"No, it's not. The poem is useless. I don't know what it means. Why, Madison? What's wrong? I haven't done anything."

"If you don't understand the poem, how about REO? *It's Time for Me to Fly.*"

"How does that apply? I'm not jealous and intolerant—if anything, you are. What is this really about? Is this about my not coming home enough? Or what? My not responding to your texts? My not reading all of yours? You know I have a lot of schoolwork. I don't have time. You can't break up with me over something so stupid. I love you, Madison. Doesn't that count for anything?"

I nod, but of course he can't see it. "I'm sorry."

"For what? Is there someone else? It's that guy at the Pansy, isn't it?"

"The heart is deceitful above all things," I say in an unintelligible mumble.

"What?"

"You broke my heart."

"How? When?"

I can't explain it to him. If I tell him that it broke my heart for him to laugh at my dreams, he'll just apologize and pretend that he can be supportive. If I tell him that I feel like I do all the work in this relationship, but he never gives back, which I already said in the poem, he'll just try to change who he is. But those kinds of changes are temporary.

I put him on a pedestal. That's not his fault, but now that I'm looking at him objectively, how can I hurt him with the truth?

"It's in the poem." What else is there to say? "I must be cruel only to be kind; Thus, bad begins and worse remains behind."

"This isn't Shakespeare, Madison. This is real. You can't just throw away what we have because you've got some stupid, romantic, emo ideas all of a sudden. I love you."

"I don't think you know me well enough to love me."

"That's bull and you know it. You know I love you."

I pull out Nathan's stupid list. "Name five things that you love about me, and they can't be physical. They have to be character traits."

I hear a sigh. "You're fun to be with." There's a long pause. "You're tenacious." There's another pause. "You're a hopeless romantic."

"I don't think *fun to be with* is a character trait, but even if I count it, that's only three things, and they could apply to lots of people. They aren't reasons to marry someone."

"Sure they are. I love all kinds of things about you. It's just hard to separate them from the physical things on the spur of the moment."

"Maybe because all we really have is the physical. But chemistry is not enough to build a marriage on."

I hate saying these things. I hate myself for hurting him, but I can't stop the flood of truth now that it's started.

"And what about the fact that we got back together based on your drug-induced haze?"

"What are you talking about?"

"I thought that you called around and found out that I was at dance camp. That you came to the Vanderbilt campus just to see me. That meant so much to me. Then I find out you stumbled across me on some kind of Ecstasy trip with your emotions all out of control."

"Who told you that?"

"It doesn't matter. The only reason I agreed to get back with you was because I thought that you had changed, but it was all a lie. You're at school partying like you did in high school, maybe getting drugs from Brett, maybe having drunken one-night stands. How would I know? You aren't honest with me.

"And I haven't been honest with you. I'm a big pretender, Cal. All I cared about inside our relationship is making you happy and planning some imaginary, romantic future. Because I loved the lie. I wanted the lie. But I wasn't looking at you so much as *us*. And we've got chemistry, and we've got things in common, but we don't agree on basic important things, and I can't pretend that it doesn't bother me anymore."

"Things like what?"

"God and children and me being a dancer."

"I'm okay with you dancing I just want you to do it at UT. And I said one or two kids would be all right. I told you I don't care if you go to church as long as you don't expect me to go with you. Those things are not big deals. You're just overreacting, like you always do. The important thing is that we get each other."

"No. We don't. I loved the you I built you up to be in my head. But you're not that person. And I loved the physical stuff and the way it made me feel wanted. I'm sorry, because I know I'm hurting you, and I never, ever wanted to hurt you, but you've hurt me too. And the damage is irreparable."

"What did I do?"

"I can't tell you."

"Why not? You're basing this whole break-up on something I did, and you won't tell me what it was? Did Brett tell you something?

Or Joey? Is it about Joey's party? I've told you that won't happen again. This is crazy!" He's yelling again. "Whatever it is, I'm sorry. Madison, don't do this!"

I'm crying so hard that I'm not sure if he understands me. "I don't want to, but I have to."

He gets quiet. It's a seething quiet. "No, you don't." His voice is like steel.

He hangs up, and I feel my heart start to harden. I put the promise ring back in its pretty little box and set it on my bedside table. But then I put it in the drawer because the condemnation coming from it is too loud. *Traitor. Heartbreaker. Heartless.*

I get dressed for work and drive there on autopilot.

Abdulla sends me out to bus tables after about fifteen minutes working the counter. "You better find your happy place before you come back," he says.

I think I need to go to the theatre for that. But I try harder to fake it. He seems satisfied.

Of course, Nathan isn't fooled. "Are you okay?"

I shake my head.

We don't have breaks at the same time, so it's not until our shifts are almost over that he talks to me again. "Do you want to tell me what happened?"

I want to tell him everything. I always want to tell him everything. Why? I haven't even told Sophie yet.

When I don't answer he says, "It's okay. You don't have to." But he looks disappointed.

"I…We… I ended it. He's not taking it well." I shrug and take a tray of salads out of the small refrigerator. He follows me to the sink and watches me drain the water out of them.

Finally, he says, "He didn't hurt you, did he?"

I'm confused for a second because, of course, he hurt me, but then I realize he means physically. "No. He wouldn't do that. Besides, he's already back at school."

"Good."

Yeah. Great.

I was too much of a coward to break up in person. Add coward to the list of words coursing through me. *Traitor. Heartbreaker. Coward.*

Nathan takes the tray from me. "Stop feeling guilty. He'll get over it."

"He didn't even see it coming."

I follow him this time as he puts the tray away, and he hands me the next one. There's a frown on his face. "What?" I ask.

"Did you feel this bad when you…back in ninth grade?"

I have to close my eyes. "Worse. You didn't do anything to deserve it."

Suddenly, the hatred I feel for myself is too overwhelming to bear. I shove the tray into his hands and run to the bathroom to throw up. I tell Abdulla I'm sick and go home.

Calvin is sitting in his car in my driveway.

Chapter Twenty-three

$\mathcal{I}$ pull past him and just sit in the car with my head on the steering wheel and wait. I don't have the energy to do this. He opens the passenger door and climbs in with a bouquet of flowers and a box.

"I didn't have time to wrap it," he says.

He looks as bad as I feel, and my heart rips a little more.

"I don't want presents. Presents won't fix this. Especially since they're bought with money you don't have."

He sighs. "Come on. You'll want this." He pushes it in my face.

I open the box and dig through newspaper and packing peanuts to find a beautiful ballerina figurine.

"It's musical too." He puts his hands over mine and twists it, and it plays a section of *Dance of the Sugar Plum Fairy.*

I pull my hands away and nearly drop it. "It's beautiful, but I wish you would take it back."

His face is twisted with pain. Tears glisten in his eyes. "I'll do anything. What do you want me to do?"

I can't bear to see him so hurt. It's breaking my heart all over again.

"There's nothing to do. You can't fix this. I've had a change of heart." I feel my own tears rolling down my face as I put the ballerina back in the box.

"You don't love me anymore? How could you just stop loving me? What's really going on?"

I don't want to say more hurtful things, but I have to. "After what we shared, I'll always love you in some way. But I think it was more the relationship that I was in love with. Over the past couple weeks, I've been taking a hard look at what I want for my future, and I don't think… We're just not very compatible. And now I don't even trust you."

"You can trust me. I'll never lie to you again. I swear it."

His eyes are killing me. I want to put my arms around him and tell him everything's going to be all right. But instead, I turn and look out the window. "I'm sorry, but—"

"You don't have to be sorry. You don't have to do this. If you still love me, and this is making you cry, and it's completely tearing my heart out, then it can't be the right thing. Please Madison, give me another chance."

I wipe my face. "It's the right thing for me. I can't spend the rest of my life with you." I grab my purse and open the door. "I'm going to go get the ring. Maybe you can get your money back for it."

I get out of the car and go to the garage door downstairs. That way, I won't run into my mom. I glance back to see him slam the ballerina figurine into the concrete of the driveway. His eyes are blazing when he looks up at me. I think he wishes that figurine was me, and for the first time, I'm scared of him. I'm frozen to the spot as he glares at me. He gets back into his car and whips out of the driveway, squealing tires and running the stop sign at the end of the block.

I get a broom from the garage and clean up the mess. It feels like I am this shattered ballerina, but I don't think I know how to put the pieces of my life back together. I've lost both dreams. Just like I was afraid of.

I hear my dad drive up as my mom calls down and asks if Calvin wants to stay for dinner. She must have seen his car when he was waiting in the driveway.

I drag myself up the stairs. My dad is walking in the back door as I come into the kitchen, so she greets him first as I lean against the door frame. I watch them kiss. Just as happy to see each other today as they were twenty-five years ago as newlyweds. That's what I want, and I couldn't have had that with Calvin.

Mom finally looks at me and frowns. "What's the matter?"

"We broke up."

She gives my dad a pointed *I-told-you-so* look and says, "Oh honey, I'm sorry."

"Good," my dad says. "I didn't like that boy. Too full of himself." If

I hadn't been so miserable, I might have laughed. Even my parents knew he wasn't right for me.

"David…" my mom says.

"He can say what he really thinks, Mom. It's not going to make me defend Calvin. It's not going to change anything."

My dad pats me on the head with the folders in his hand. "Good."

I give him a hug.

"I'm sorry if you're sad," he says, "but you're too young to date anyone seriously anyway." He goes to his office to put his stuff away.

He's right about that, too. But I did let it get too serious, and now it's destroyed me.

My mom is biting her lip, looking at me like she might look at a deer in her headlights. Maybe I look as shattered as I feel. "Don't fix anything for me. I'm not hungry."

I go back downstairs to my room and call Sophie. After I tell her about the breakup, practically twice since I'm crying so hard that I have to repeat most of it, she has the decency not to gloat.

"I'm sorry you're hurting. Maybe the way to stop feeling guilty and sad is to move on—to Nathan," she says.

"Nathan has zero interest in a relationship with me. I slammed that door tight in ninth grade. Besides, we don't have anything in common. He likes outdoorsy stuff, and he hunts, and he listens to country music."

"There must be a reason he's being so nice to you."

"He's just a nice guy. And I think he just really hates Calvin because of the whole strike incident."

"Don't we all. But you do have things in common with the pompous…with Calvin, and that didn't really matter in the long run."

"What are you saying?"

"Just don't rule Nathan out."

I get sixteen texts from Calvin before I go to sleep. It's all basically the same thing he said in the car. Stuff like:

 Sorry I lost my temper. ILY

 I'll buy you another dancer. ILY

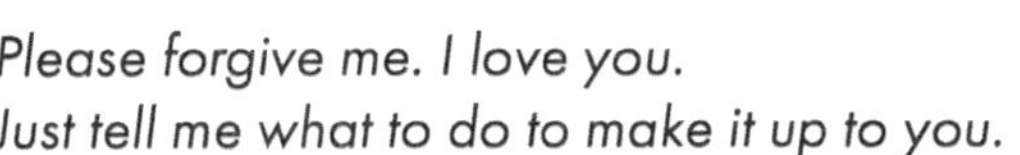

Please forgive me. I love you.
Just tell me what to do to make it up to you.

I don't answer any of them. What is there to say? There is nothing he can do. He doesn't support my dream of dancing and owning a studio someday. He doesn't want to have kids. Most importantly, he doesn't even believe in God. He lies to me. He told lies about me to his friends. The list is endless. Now that I can see it, I can't believe I didn't see it *before* I slept with him. And I can't forgive myself for that.

That stupid voice in my head, all that poetry, was shouting at me to open my eyes, and I squeezed them tighter instead. I'm so stupid. And weak. And sinful.

I check online. He has posted all kinds of stuff. It's embarrassing. Now all my friends know I broke up with him and probably think I'm heartless for not making up with him.

I delete what I can.

I toss and turn all night. Maybe I should tell him what he did that broke my heart. But he would support anything right now. I could tell him I want to move to Pakistan and be a female wrestler, and he'd probably help me pack as long as I took him with me. Can I really ignore that kind of loyalty, that kind of love?

I have to.

It's not real.

It's born out of his desperation, his emptiness. He loved me because I put him on a pedestal, not because of who I am. I didn't let him see who I really am because I wanted him to make me feel loved and wanted. What a vicious, dysfunctional, toxic cycle that has left me feeling horrible and heartless.

Because I had sex with him. He knew what that meant to me— the commitment it represented. And then, only two weeks later, I blindsided him with a breakup.

How can I forgive myself for that? How can God forgive me?

My phone buzzes in my pocket a billion times at work on Friday. More texts. More apologies. More empty promises. I've got circles under my eyes, and they are red and puffy from crying. To say I look like the living dead would be a compliment.

My sister brings Kaitlyn by the Pansy for an early supper. She watches me carefully as I ring up her order. She knows. Mom must have told her. She finally says, "If you weren't even sure that you loved him, why are you taking this so hard?"

I hand her my phone. She scans through the texts. "Wow. You really broke his heart."

I have to close my eyes and mash my lips together and think about the way he laughed at me to keep from crying. When I pull myself together, I say, "He broke mine first."

"What'd he do? Cheat on you? There are a lot of apologies here." She hands me my phone back.

I shake my head. "You said not to marry a man who didn't support my dreams. He laughed. He said they were pipe dreams."

She motions for me to come out from behind the counter. There's only one other customer in the place, and he already has his pizza, so I go.

She hugs me tightly. "Well, I thought you should break up with him, anyway, because he's not a Christian. So, I'm glad. I think you did the right thing."

"It doesn't feel like it."

She puts her hand under my face and lifts my chin. "When you are in City Ballet Company Two, you'll know it was right."

"And if I don't make it? If it really is a pipe dream? I didn't even get the scholarship for the classes."

"No. None of that talk."

Kaitlyn parrots her. "No."

For the first time all day, I smile. I carry a highchair to the table for them. As they are sitting, Nathan comes out with a helium balloon for Kaitlyn, and she squeals with delight. I introduce Nathan to my sister.

"Haven't I seen you somewhere before?" Kayleigh asks him.

"I don't think so."

She narrows her eyes at him then looks at me and points her finger. "He's in that picture in your room."

My eyes grow wide. I can't believe she remembers that. The picture she's talking about is from the ninth-grade homecoming dance. It's in a silver frame, and I printed out the words *First Love* and stuck it in there. I've had it on my bookcase since I got it, but I stuck it in a drawer when I started dating Calvin. Nathan's looking at me questioningly. "I've just got some old snapshots on my bulletin board. I'm surprised she recognized you."

That's not a lie. He is in the collage of photos on my bulletin board. But you have to look really hard.

Kaitlyn starts to cry because somehow, she has managed to untie the balloon. It's floating to the ceiling. I grab the string just in time. Kayleigh is grinning at me.

"He's the necklace guy?" she asks.

Nathan is crouched next to the highchair making some sort of childproof slip knot thingy and talking baby talk to Kaitlyn, so I'm hoping he didn't hear. I give her an angry, pointed look, begging her with my eyes not to go there.

Nathan stands. "Necklace guy?"

"Our parents were in a golf tournament in the middle of nowhere," she tells him. "And they rented a cabin—and I use the term loosely. We thought it was going to be a snazzy resort and Derrick and I went with them. Madison brought Sophie along."

I feel my face burning. "Kayleigh," I warn. She ignores me.

"The cabin was a real dump, and the bathroom had this rusty, pedestal sink that didn't have a stopper. Well, Madison had this ballerina necklace that she never took off except for dance class and showers."

Nathan looks at me, surprised. He knows it's the necklace he gave me for Christmas when we were together, but hopefully he'll think this happened that same year.

"When was this?" he asks me.

Ugh! I really want to lie. Before I can stammer out a reply, Kayleigh says, "Just a little over a year ago?" She looks at me. "I was very pregnant. I remember that."

"We really should get back to work," I say to Nathan.

"You go ahead. I want to hear the rest of the story." He grins at my embarrassment.

"Well, she took the necklace off," Kayleigh continues, "and took a shower. But when she got out, she was wiping the mirror with the towel and the bottom of it hit the necklace and knocked in into the sink and down the drain." Kayleigh starts laughing. "You would not believe the scream. We thought she was being murdered. She started crying so hard it took ten minutes to get the story out of her. Luckily, Derrick was able to take the sink apart and get it back for her."

She shakes her head. "I thought we were going to have to sedate her." She takes a sip of her soda and leans toward Kaitlyn. "Auntie Madison lost her mind," she says in baby talk and Kaitlyn giggles.

I give her my best death glare. "Thanks for that." I don't even look at Nathan as I go back to work. I wish I could just leave.

He stops me in the kitchen with this big, goofy grin on his face. "Fair is fair," he says and reaches in his back pocket and pulls out a ratty, leather wallet. The wallet I gave him for Christmas that year? It's falling apart.

He shrugs. "I couldn't throw it out. My mom has tried to give me three different new ones." He shoves it back in his pocket and goes to the ovens to get Kayleigh's pizza.

I unload the dishwasher in the kitchen. I remember the necklace incident because it was a turning point. Sophie told me in her not-so-subtle way that I was never going to move on and have another real relationship if I kept holding on to one that I purposely discarded.

"I get it now," she had said. "I've set you up with at least ten different guys since you broke up with Nathan and none of them were ever good enough. Too short, too stupid, too vulgar, too into cars, too into sports, only interested in sex—good grief. It's always something."

"I'm picky. So what? I don't have to have a boyfriend anyway."

"But you broke all those guys' hearts. They all liked you. Every one. But you never gave them a chance. Four or five dates tops."

I was getting angry. "What is your point?"

"I get it now. You've been comparing everyone to Nathan." She looked so smug. "You've got to let the boy go. That's ancient history. Give someone a real chance."

Three weeks later I met Calvin. He made me laugh. He was a good kisser. I put the necklace in my jewelry box and took her advice.

Now look at me. Will I ever choose wisely? My eyes fill with tears.

The house is empty when I get home. There's a note on the refrigerator saying they've gone to a dinner party. I eat some leftovers and try to read, but I can't focus. There's a knock at the back door.

It's Calvin.

I want to pretend I'm not home, but he can see me through the sheer curtain on the door's window.

He starts pounding. "Madison, come on. Let me in."

I open the door, and he pushes his way in. "About time," he says.

"Why are you here?"

He's smirking, with his chin up, so confident. Not like he was last time I saw him.

"I figured out what this is all about." His words are slow and a little slurred.

"What?"

He points back and forth between us. "This little break up thing."

"Little break up thing?"

"You're just going through a phase, like I did. Maybe we moved too fast, and it threw you, or maybe it's just senioritis, it doesn't matter. I just came to tell you that I understand, and I'll be waiting for you when you get over it." His face is calm and hopeful.

"I'm not going to get over it. I'm not coming back to you. I've made up my mind."

His face turns to stone. He grabs me and kisses me, but I don't kiss him back. He reeks of beer. "Oh, you are going to kiss me," he says and pushes me onto the couch.

"Calvin, stop it." I try to get up but his grip on my arms is like a vice.

"You like it. I know you do. If it's not a phase, then it's about the sex." He pushes me down to my back and leans over me. "You finally give it up to me, so now you're ready to give it to everyone. Like your friend at the Pansy. Well, he can't have you. You're mine." He smashes his lips against mine.

I turn my face away. "You're hurting me." I try to squirm out of his grasp, so he puts a knee on my leg.

"Oh, I'm so sorry. I never wanted to hurt you," he says with mock sympathy. "Does that make you feel better?"

I don't say anything. It makes me feel like dirt.

"Yeah. It didn't do anything for me either." He takes my wrists in one hand and puts them over my head and rips my shirt open. Buttons go flying everywhere.

"You're drunk. You don't know what you're doing. Please stop this." I try to buck him off my leg and his knee slips and pinches my skin. "Ow. Get off my leg." The pain brings tears to my eyes, but the way he's acting is worse than the pain.

"I ought to break your leg. Both your legs. Then you won't care about dancing more than me." He runs a hand up and down my leg. "I could, you know. I could snap it in two." There's a scary look on his face, like when he broke the figurine. I'm starting to believe he might really hurt me. My phone is out of reach on the end table. Panic swells up in me.

"Or maybe we could start making babies now. That's what you want, right?" He reaches to unbuckle his pants. "You won't leave me if you're pregnant."

"Please stop. Cal, please. You're not thinking straight."

"Shut up!" He looks into my eyes and sees the fear there.

The anger changes to defeat in his eyes. He lets go of my wrists and lies down on top of me with his head on my chest. His shoulders shake from crying. I put my arms around him and let him.

"I'm so sorry I've hurt you," I say. "It's going to be okay. We're not good for each other. You need someone who will love you for you. I'm not that person."

He sits up with a scowl and wipes his face. "Don't tell me what I need." His voice comes out like a growl. He grabs my arms again and shakes me. "I need you! Don't you understand? I was willing to do anything for you. I even sold drugs for you."

"What?"

"I didn't cash in bonds. I've been selling drugs for Brett, so I can have enough money to take you out and buy you things. But do you appreciate it? No!" He shoves me hard and then stands. "You don't appreciate anything I do. You're selfish and heartless! You don't even deserve me." He storms out of the house.

Chapter Twenty-four

$\mathcal{I}$ must be numb. Or maybe I'm all out of tears. I find most of the buttons and sit on the end of my bed and painstakingly sew them back on. A couple of the buttonholes are torn. I don't know what to do about that. It's my work shirt. A short-sleeved, dark purple, button-down. I have two and alternate days. When I finish, it looks terrible. I throw it in the trash.

I take off my clothes to shower and look at myself in my ballet mirror. There's a huge bruise coming on the inside of my thigh, and handprint-shaped marks on my upper arms. My wrists are still red, but I don't think they'll bruise. I'm glad it's winter so I can cover it all up.

After I shower, I crawl in my bed and curl up in a ball. I know in my head that what he did was wrong, but my heart keeps whispering *heartbreaker, heartless, coward*, and the new mantra: *You deserved it. You deserved it.*

I don't sleep much. But the voice in my head is too filled with condemnation to spout poetry. Around six in the morning I get a text from an unknown number:

> *Cal's in the hospital because of you. Hope you're*
> *happy. Lyla*

His sister. I text back:

> *What happened? Is he going to be okay?*

She doesn't respond for a long, long time. I'm about ready to go to the hospital and find out for myself when she finally texts back:

> *Car accident. He has a concussion. Don't come.*
> *He doesn't want to see you.*

He was drunk when he left here. I shouldn't have let him drive. I should have taken him home. He could've been killed. He could have killed someone. The knife of guilt in my stomach twists painfully.

I stay in bed all day Saturday and Sunday. I don't even go to church. What difference does it make? I'm so stupid. I asked for one sign. And I got tons of them, but I was too blind to see them. They were there all along. Cal's behavior which should have counteracted his words; my sister telling me to marry a man who supports my dreams, and that I shouldn't even date a non-believer, let alone marry one; my mom telling me to marry a man who treats his mom well—not like a servant; Sophie telling me he wasn't right for me and talking about settling and how I wasn't myself around Cal; Kendra saying I was lying to myself about who he was.

And Nathan. So many signs from Nathan.

But I couldn't see any of them through my walls made of happily-ever-after.

I can forgive Calvin for attacking me—not that he's asking for my forgiveness now—he's too mad at me for breaking his heart. But I don't know how to forgive myself for giving in to the physical, letting go of my standards, letting go of my dreams of being in the company because of stupid Celeste who wasn't a sign at all. She didn't even take notes at the audition. She probably knew about Megan's situation and had made up her mind before she even showed up to judge.

I gave my virginity away to a boy I'm not going to marry. Now I'm not worthy of the kind of guy I want to marry. A guy like Nathan. Who's waiting. And wants someone who is waiting too.

The worst part, though, is knowing that God did give me all the signs I begged for to make the right decision, and I broke His heart, too. I'm not worthy of His love either.

At dance team, I cover up my bruised arms with a ballet sweater. I didn't even tell Sophie what Calvin did. There's no telling what she'd do. I wear a lightweight, long-sleeved shirt under my work shirt all week.

Everyone at the Pansy is buzzing about Rick's birthday party on

Saturday. It's an all day and night affair so everyone can come for some of it, even if they have to work. Even Abdulla said he's going for a little while. My parents are going to some timeshare resort for the weekend where it's warm so they can play golf, and I'm nervous about being in the house alone, but I don't really feel like partying.

I think Calvin has gone back to school, but I don't know for sure. I don't know anything. Did he get a DUI? Was someone else hurt in the accident? Have they pressed charges? Is this going to ruin his future? If it does, that'll pour more gasoline on my guilt inferno.

Nathan keeps his distance. He should. He kept the wallet I gave him, but I don't know what that means. It could mean that he really doesn't hate me. It could mean that I would have had a chance with him if I'd broken up with Cal when he asked me to. But now, too much has happened. The distance feels meaningful, though. Like it's his way of saying he doesn't even want to be friends anymore. Maybe I don't deserve even that.

"Madison, there's going to be dancing at my party," Rick says to me in the kitchen on Friday. "And three kegs," he whispers. "You're coming, aren't you?"

"I don't think so."

He takes my hand and puts an arm around my waist and sways back and forth. "Come on. There'll be dancing." He leads me around in a circle. "I'm a good dancer. Word is you dumped the crappy boyfriend. The guys are going to start lining up, and I want to be at the front of the line." Rick is several years older than me, but he has such a baby face. He's kind of adorable. Especially when he smiles, like now. That's how he gets away with his inappropriate behavior. He leans in close to my ear. "I won't take no for an answer." Then he dips me.

It surprises a laugh out of me. It's the first time all week that I've laughed. It makes me feel so much better that I think maybe partying is a good idea after all. Actually, getting a little drunk seems like a good idea, too. I've never done it before, but maybe that's just what I need. I can just laugh and dance and forget about all this drama for a little while. Let it go.

I don't want to feel like this anymore.

"You are a good dancer," I say and turn on some of that flirt I've developed from talking to Ken every day. "I'll only come if you promise to dance with me."

"It's a deal." He steps back and twirls me around, and I can't help but remember when Nathan did that in the parking lot. I glance over at him. He's watching us with a frown.

I don't care. I'm never going to be good enough for him. Maybe I should try not being so hard on myself and have some fun.

I did what I did. I can't turn into a zombie over it.

What's gone and what's past help should be past grief.

I put on my turquoise mini-dress for the party. It's clingy and just long enough to cover up the bruise. Normally, I would wear it with leggings, but I'm feeling not-normal. Besides, I have to wear a sweater to cover up my arms, and I'll get hot dancing. The dress is low cut, but I don't have any cleavage, so it's not revealing. I wear black heels with ankle straps. My legs are my one good feature. I might as well show them off.

I've pre-arranged with Sophie to take me and pick me up so I can drink. She wants to stay and see this bizarre event in person, but she has to work.

"I'm not a fan of this plan. Especially after what happened with the margaritas. But you've had my back after I've partied, so I won't let you down. When you get to the point that everything is funny, you need to stop," she counsels. "Otherwise, you'll be puking, and that ruins everything."

"I'm only going to have two drinks. I do not want to throw up, do something I'll regret, or have a hangover tomorrow."

She gives me a quick hug before I get out of the car. "My little Madison going to her first big girl party."

I roll my eyes. "Shut up. Text me when you get off work, and I'll come outside and wait."

"Okay."

It's a big house, and the bass from the music is shaking the whole thing. It's music so loud I can get lost inside it. Perfect.

According to the signs, it's Rick's twenty-first birthday. At least he'll be drinking legally. Thankfully, I find the kitchen stocked with more than just the keg since the smell of beer brings back things that I don't want to think about. There are some bottles of hard lemonade on the counter, and I take one and search for the music which seems to be coming from upstairs. I down my drink as I walk toward the music like I'm magnetized.

There are probably thirty people in this huge rec room. There's a pool table shoved to the side so there's plenty of room for dancing. I toss my empty bottle and push myself into the crowd and start dancing.

When a slow song comes on, I can't bear being so alone in the sea of couples and go get another drink. There's a punch bowl. It's definitely spiked, and I choke on my first sip, but then I gulp it down like bad medicine and toss my cup.

An arm lands on my shoulder. "Pace yourself," a familiar voice says. Ken. I didn't expect to see him here. But I don't know half the people I've seen.

Ken wasn't named best-looking for nothing. Creamy brown skin, short, black curls and those hazel eyes that absolutely put me in a trance. I'm surprised I don't start drooling. His eyes roam up and down my body, lingering on my legs. "You look exceptionally hot tonight. How about a dance? Or…," he looks around, "do you still have a boyfriend?"

I shake my head and put my arm through his. "I'm all yours."

"Excellent."

We dance close for the remainder of the slow song and then bump and grind our way through several fast songs. He's got a broader chest and way more muscles than Calvin, and I'm betting he looks amazing without his shirt. When we're swaying to another slow song, he leans in to kiss me. There's a reason I shouldn't kiss him tickling my brain, and I pull back slightly.

Rick swoops in and pulls me away from Ken. "Save some for me," he says. "You promised me a dance."

Ken tries to pull me back, "Snooze you lose, birthday boy."

I give him an apologetic smile. "I did promise him."

Rick hands me another cup of punch. *What number am I on? Only my third, right? Won't hurt to have three.* When I finish, we start dancing. I'm having a blast. He does all kinds of swing moves with turns and dips. When the music slows down, he switches to a close rhumba and leans in and kisses my neck. The dancing has already made me feel incredible—or maybe it's the drinks. Whatever. I'm fine. He kisses me, and I'm actually wondering about what it would be like to do more than kiss. My virginity is gone. What difference does it make now? I might as well do what makes me happy.

Everybody else does.

I wonder if that's the alcohol talking. I don't feel drunk, but I know this isn't Normal-Madison behavior. I guess it's Not-Normal-Madison behavior. That's who I am tonight: Not-Normal-Madison. She's a little red corvette. A laugh bubbles up at the thought.

I arch back and Rick's lips move down my throat. I open my eyes and see an upside-down Nathan glaring at me from across the room. I stand straight and tell Rick that I'm ready for a break.

"We could go to my room," he says in my ear.

Nathan shouts over the music. "Madison? What are you doing?"

I giggle and put an arm on his shoulder. "I'm just dancing. Do you want to dance with me?"

Nathan is still frowning. Why doesn't he lighten up? It's a party. "Are you drunk?"

"Maybe. I don't know. I've never been drunk before. I don't think I am." I look at Rick. "Am I?"

"Oh, yeah." He grins, and I giggle again. "And I think we were just going to my room, so beat it Ford."

"We were? But Nathan's here. Hi, Nathan."

Nathan pulls me away from Rick. "That's not going to happen."

"I'm going to dance with Nathan now," I tell Rick. I put both arms around Nathan's neck and put my head on his chest. We sway back and forth for a minute. "You're a lot bigger than you were at homecoming. I lift my head up and kiss his neck. I can just reach it with my two-inch heels on. He seems very uncomfortable with my body pressed against his. Not like Rick or Ken who couldn't seem to pull me close enough.

"Why don't I take you home?" he says.

"But you just got here."

"No, I've been here awhile." He says it very seriously. I should call him Mr. Serious, but somehow, I don't think he'll think that's as funny as I do.

"Sophie's supposed to come get me." I pull my cell from my sweater pocket. Only ten-thirty. "I've got loads of time. She's closing."

I want to see him smile. "Come on, dance with me a little. Let's have some fun."

He holds me a little tighter, and I relax against him. We sway back and forth for a few minutes, then he lets out this tremendous sigh. "I want to do the right thing here."

I make a pouty face. "Don't be a party pooper."

"Let me take you home."

I move my face as close to his as I can. "So you can have me all to yourself?" I try to kiss him, but he pulls his head back.

"I'm trying to stop you from doing something stupid."

"Something else, you mean?" I laugh. "I think that ship has sailed, mate. I am the Queen of Stupidville." I tug at my sweater. "It's hot in here. I think I need another drink."

"We'll get you a bottled water on the way out." He puts his arm around me and guides me to the door.

"Hey Ford," Rick shouts, "you owe me for getting her warmed up for you." Nathan shoots him a death glare, and I giggle some more. I guess I *am* drunk. Sophie said when everything is funny then I've had enough.

The cool night air feels good. Nathan makes sure I'm buckled in before he closes the door and goes to the driver's side. The water tastes way better than that disgusting punch that I forced down. Why did I do that? So I could feel stupid and thick? And make Mr. Serious mad at me again?

Tears stream down my face from nowhere. There is something seriously wrong with me.

"What's wrong?" Nathan asks because *he's* the kind of guy that notices. *He's* the kind of guy I want to marry. *He's* got all the qualities I want.

"I'm damaged goods."

"Don't say that."

"It's true. Only sleazy guys will ever be interested in me now. And I don't want to get HPV."

He tries to hide a smile, but I don't see what's so funny. "HPV? What are you talking about?" he asks.

"Ken has HPV. Sleazy guys have STDs."

"Then why were you kissing them?"

"Maybe that's all I'm good for now. And gilded honour shamefully misplaced, And maiden virtue rudely strumpeted, And right perfection wrongfully disgraced. Yep. Strumpeted virtue." That word is hilarious. "*Rudely* strumpeted." I start laughing, but the sad fact of those words turns the water works back on.

At a stop light, he reaches over and opens the glove compartment and hands me a small box of tissues from it. "Stop it, Madison. You're taking this guilt trip too far."

I dab my eyes.

"Either it means everything, or it means nothing. Either I'm damaged goods, or I lose my standards, so I can live with myself and go on."

"Or you admit that you made a mistake, and you decide not to make it again."

I think about that for a few minutes, but it's hard to focus. Why did I want to get drunk anyway? "I don't know how to do that. It's easier to just accept that I have no standards. It's more fun too. Not-Normal-Madison is way more fun than zombie Madison, don't you think?"

"You never struck me as someone who takes the easy way out."

I sigh and blow my nose. And then I start giggling because of the noise my nose makes. "I think I'm a little drunk."

"No kidding."

"I'm a coward. If I was brave…if I just…my whole life would have turned out differently." I want to say that if I'd been brave, I never would have cheated on him, because I would have stood up to Sophie and not gone on the double date in the first place.

"You say that like your life is over. You're seventeen."

I think about that. Well, I try to. And I realize something. My happily ever after is not dependent on having a relationship in my life right now. Who needs the drama? "I'm seventeen. My life has just begun," I say really loud.

"Okay."

"I don't need a relationship. I have plenty of time for that someday." Maybe someday there'll be another guy like Nathan, who I'll have the courage to love. At least now I know what I want in a guy.

We go through McDonald's drive-thru. "Do you want any food? Or just coffee?"

"Mmmm. Caramel-Mocha coffee. Warm." My little sweater just isn't cutting it now.

It's too hot to drink at first, so I just let it keep my hands warm.

He pulls up in my driveway and the big, empty house looms over us like the grim reaper. I glance around to make sure my car is the only one here. "Thanks for being a friend to me tonight when I obviously disgust you."

He sort of chuckles. "Why do you think that?"

"You've barely said two words to me all week. I figured you'd had enough of the drama, drama, drama of the Queen of Stupidville."

"I was trying to give you some time."

My phone buzzes in my pocket. I hand Nathan my coffee. "Oh, I forgot to tell Sophie that she doesn't have to pick me up."

But it's not Sophie.

It's a picture of me dancing with Ken, a picture of Rick kissing my neck, and a picture of me walking out the door with Nathan's arm around me. It buzzes again with this message from Cal:

> *I was going to come apologize. But you're prob-*
> *ably still with guy number three. I'm posting these.*

Chapter Twenty-five

*I*ve read in books where people say the blood drained from their face, but I'd never actually experienced it until this moment. I may throw up now.

"What is it?" Nathan asks.

"Did you see Calvin at the party?"

"No, but I saw his friend Joey. Why?"

"What's wrong with me? Why do I keep screwing up?"

He takes the phone out of my hand. I feel like that shattered figurine again. I lay my head back on the seat. "I thought he got it out of his system last week."

"You said he was at school."

"He came back. He was waiting for me when I got home that day and then…" I shake my head. "Never mind. I don't want to talk about it. I don't want to think about it. Oh! That's why I wanted to get drunk. I knew there had to be a reason."

I take the phone and the coffee back. The coffee is yummy and soothing, and I just sit there and drink it. Nathan's probably wondering why I don't go inside, but I'm afraid to be home alone now that I know Calvin's in town. I don't think he'll come over—but I never thought he'd attack me either. Being drunk makes him mean. Like his dad. What if he's drunk now?

"Could you come in for a little while?" I ask.

"Where are your parents?"

I take another sip. "Out of town."

"I don't think it's a good idea."

I nod. "It's okay. I'll ask Sophie. She doesn't care that I'm stupid. She's stupid sometimes too." I text her that I'm home and ask her to come 911.

"What was he going to apologize for?"

I grab another tissue from the glove box and shake my head. I don't want to tell him. "Could you just stay until she gets here?"

"Are you afraid he's going to come over? Did he hurt you?"

"He didn't mean it. He was drunk. I thought maybe he was back at school or still in the hospital or maybe even in jail, since I haven't heard from him all week, but I guess he's still in town. And if Joey sent him those pictures, he's probably pretty mad. I bet Joey teased him. He's such a jerk."

"Did you press charges? Is that why you thought he was in jail?"

"No. He had a car accident, but I don't know if anyone else was involved. I don't really know anything about it, but it happened after he left here. His sister texted me about it. She hates me too. I should start a club. You can be president if you want."

"How many times do I have to tell you that I don't hate you?"

"I'm a nightmare. Run for your life." I open the door, but he grabs my arm right on the bruise. I wince.

"I'm sorry." He lets go. "Did that hurt?"

I don't answer. I just head for the door to the garage because it's closest and it's freezing out here. I'm really regretting the no leggings decision. And I can't seem to get the stupid key in the lock.

Nathan takes it from me and opens the door. "I'll stay until Sophie gets here."

I go in the bathroom and nearly scare myself when I look in the mirror. My mascara has formed black circles under my eyes. I wash what's left of my make up off. How did Nathan keep a straight face with my zombie-street-walker-from-the-apocalypse look?

Pity. That's how.

My sweats are in my bedroom and so is Nathan. He's looking at the collage of pictures on my bulletin board.

"I find it really hard to believe your sister recognized me from this tiny picture."

I open my dresser drawer and pull out the homecoming picture and set it on top, but don't say anything. I get my sweats out of my closet and pull off my heels and hang up my sweater.

"Did he do that to you?" He's staring at my arms.

Crud. I forgot. I slip the sweatshirt on over my dress.

"That's why you've been in long sleeves all week at work," he says.

I cross my arms over my chest and stare at the floor.

"What happened?"

"Nothing. He tried to…but he couldn't go through with it." I lift my eyes to see his reaction. "He's angrier now, I bet, because of those pictures. What if…"

Nathan crosses the room in about three steps and puts his arms around me. "It's okay. I won't let him touch you." He runs his hand slowly and so gently down the back of my head. I lean into him. He smells good, and he feels good, and I feel very safe for the first time since that night. I know he'll protect me.

I hear the door from the garage open and tense up. Nathan's arms tighten around me, but then Sophie's voice booms in the quiet, "Okay, I'm here. What's the big emergency and whose car is that in—?" She sees us, and we quickly pull apart. "Oh." She's looking at me skeptically, then she grins. "You have Nathan in your bedroom, and this is an emergency because…?"

I run over and hug her. "You came. Can you stay over?"

"Doesn't look like you need me to stay over."

"Very funny. I've told you a million times Nathan is not interested in me."

"Yeah. I can see that."

"Calvin really hates me, though, and that's why I need you to stay. It's on my phone." I go to the bathroom to get my phone. And remember the coffee in there too. I finish it off in a few gulps to fortify myself before showing Sophie the spectacular mess I made of things. When I come back there's some quiet conversation going on.

"Show me your arms," she says.

I frown at Nathan. "I wasn't going to tell her that part. Isn't this bad enough?" I hand her my phone.

She flips through the pictures. "Good grief, Madison. What were you thinking?"

"I didn't want to think." I sit down on my bed. "I just wanted to get lost in the music."

"Show me your arms." I take off my sweatshirt. "Holy cow! And why didn't you tell me this?"

"He had an accident. I figured he suffered enough without the wrath of Sophie." I wiggle my fingers dramatically.

She narrows her eyes at me. "Oh, there's going to be some wrath. What else did he do?"

I lift my dress and show her the bruise on my thigh. "That's all. He didn't go through with it. He was drunk. People do stupid things when they're drunk." I fall back on my bed. "Obviously."

"Do not defend him," Nathan says coldly.

Sophie starts looking through the texts on my phone. "This is seriously stalkerish. And who the heck is this Lyla chick?"

"His sister. And he quit sending the texts. I thought maybe he'd given up."

"You've got to tell me exactly what happened. I think you should press charges or at least get a restraining order."

"I don't want to think about it."

Nathan sits down next to me. "Maybe, considering your condition, it would be easier to talk about it now. And maybe talking about it will help you process it. You're obviously still upset."

"My condition?" This throws me for a minute. "Oh. The drunk thing. Yeah." I picture Cal's face looming over me and shudder. "No."

"Do you want Nathan to leave?" Sophie asks.

I frown, confused. "Why would I want him to leave? I can tell him anything."

"So tell me," he says.

I sit up with a sigh. "Okay."

I tell them the whole story, starting with the ballerina figurine on Thursday.

"I wish that pompous pinhead would come over here," Sophie says when I'm done. "I'd break every bone in his body." Her whole face is blazing with fury. Tiny little Sophie. Made of tiger.

I grin at Nathan, but he looks just as furious. "I'd help," he says.

She throws her purse on my bed and rubs her face with her hands. "Okay. First things first. We check the damage. Where's your computer?"

While we wait for my laptop to come on, she tells me to stand up and takes my picture. Then she makes me lift up the dress for a picture of the big bruise.

"What are you doing this for?"

"Leverage."

Nathan stands up. "I think you're in good hands. I'm going to go." He picks up my phone and taps in his number, then asks for mine and puts it in his phone. "Call me if you need to talk."

"I'll walk you out." I take his arm and walk quietly beside him. I don't really have anything to tell him, I just want to be close to him as long as I can. When he comes to his senses tomorrow, he'll remember I'm damaged, and he's not into stupid.

"I like your Shakespeare wall. You've got a pretty nice set up in your room for working out," he says.

"Yeah. My dad is awesome."

"Have you told him about the company auditions?"

"No. I've kind of been busy having a nuclear meltdown."

"It might be a good time to have something new to focus on."

"You're right, as usual." I hug him and say into his chest, "I keep screwing up, and you keep saving me. Thanks for still being my friend, even though I'm so stupid, and damaged, and unforgivably heartless and cowardly."

He steps back from my hug, and I'm sure he's repulsed, but he lifts my chin up. "I think you're smart, and talented, and your heart is too big for your own good. But I also think that you need to forgive yourself." He strokes my cheek with his thumb. "Do you believe that God can forgive you for anything?"

"Yes. But…"

"No buts. As far as the east is from the west that's how far He removes our transgressions from us. Let it go, Maddy. Start fresh. God can help. Turn it over to Him. His opinion is the only one that matters."

I think he's going to kiss me. He looks at my lips like he wants to, but then he doesn't.

He's a smart guy.

"Goodnight, Madison Beth."

When I get back to my room, Sophie is in full-on revenge mode. "Okay. It's pretty bad."

I look over her shoulder. He has captioned the pictures: *Guess you dumped me to sleep around. You didn't waste time.*

Lovely. He's tagged everyone he can in the pictures too.

"I sent him the pictures of you and told him that if he didn't remove the party pictures, we were going to post the pictures of the bruises with a full explanation and then press charges of attempted rape."

I pull off my dress and put on my sweats. "I'm going to get some ice cream. You want some?"

She's frowning at me. Probably because of my lack of enthusiasm. "Do you know his email and password? I want to set it so that the pictures only show up on his wall. That way he won't realize they're gone if I delete them. But I'll have to un-tag everyone. Hmmm…" She mumbles some more about what she wants to do.

I write down the email address for her. "He probably changed his password. It was Madslovesme—all one word. But before that it was Einstein69. I guess you can try both. Ice cream?"

"Mads. *Ugh!* I hate that nickname." She shakes her head as she types it in. I grin because I never liked it either, but she takes my grin the wrong way and gets more worked up. "This is serious. He is completely destroying your reputation here, and he attacked you. Why aren't you more upset?"

"Uh, I think *I* destroyed my reputation by acting like that at the party. And what he did to me was because he was hurt and angry."

"Are you serious?"

I'm so tired. I lean against the desk. "He was drunk. He wasn't himself."

"No. He was mad at you and wanted to hurt you. He *purposely* hurt you."

"I don't think he came here with the intent of hurting me. He lost his temper because of the drinking."

"You are unbelievable! First you keep this from me and then you keep defending him. What is wrong with you? He threatened *rape*. Do you even get that?"

I shake my head and put my hands over my ears. I'm too tired of thinking about this. I'm too tired to think at all.

But she keeps pestering me. She pulls my hands away from my ears. "Madison. Please. He is *so* not worthy of your defense. What he did was inexcusable. Unforgivable. Criminal! You have got to stand up for yourself."

"Maybe I deserved it!" It feels good to scream the words that have been pounding in my head all week.

I've never seen Sophie speechless before. She sits back down at the desk with this look of total shock on her face. The quiet in the room hurts my ears. Finally, she says, "That's what you think?"

I don't answer.

"Why?"

The words slowly seep out of me like pus from a wound. "I told him I loved him. I made the ultimate commitment to him by sleeping with him. I took his pre-engagement ring and then, two weeks later, I threw it all back in his face. He didn't deserve that. He never saw it coming. It was the ultimate betrayal. Just like with Nathan. I'm a stupid, blind, heartless idiot, and I deserve their hatred." I throw myself on my bed. "I deserve much worse."

She doesn't say anything for the longest time, and I start to doze off.

"Why did you break up with him?" Her words startle me. "I was really surprised you did that after you slept with him. Especially after our talk about waiting. You convinced me not to, and what? I talked you out of waiting? I'm so sorry, Maddy."

Talked her out of it; talked myself into it. Ironic.

"Wasn't your fault. It happened when I got back from the theatre after Celeste destroyed my hope. I was feeling so empty. I thought it would help.

"But I broke up with him because of what my sister said and Nathan's stupid list." I roll over, sit up, and cross my legs. She's waiting for me to explain. "I couldn't name five things that weren't physical that I loved about him. Then I came up with a list of the things that I wanted in a future husband, and I realized Calvin didn't have any of them. None. But it was too late. I'd already committed to him.

"So, then I tried to look at him objectively, and I didn't like what I saw. You were right. He was pompous and selfish and spoiled, and I was not myself around him. And Nathan was right. I was just overlooking all of his faults because I wanted to prove that I could be in a committed relationship. I was in love with being in love and some crazy idea I had about marriage and living happily ever after. Because I just wanted everything all planned out." I prop my head on my hands. "I found out he wasn't even reading most of my texts, and then he wasn't honest about where he got the money for the ring. I tried to be happy, but I couldn't. I didn't even trust him anymore. Then I gave him the ultimate test and he failed."

"What test?"

Telling Sophie seems like a good trial run for telling my parents. "I don't want to go to UT and major in Education. I want to try out for City Ballet's Company Two and be in their program with Bell-meade College. And after I dance with them for a few years, I want to open a dance studio and teach." Her eyes widen, but she doesn't say anything. "He laughed at me. Said I wasn't good enough, and that it was a pipe dream." The tears come to my eyes just thinking about it, but I blink them away. "That was the deal breaker."

"Did you tell him that?"

I'm amazed at her restraint in not commenting. "I can't tell him. He'll say anything to get me back. That was his gut reaction, and it wasn't the right one."

She nods. "You did what was right for you. The big commitment"—she puts air quotes around it—"was only for two weeks. That's not so bad. If you'd left him at the altar, it still wouldn't mean you were heartless, but it would be a lot worse. The point is you had to get out of the relationship. He is responsible for his own pain and the way he deals with that. Let him be responsible."

She crawls across the bed and hugs me. "Stop with the guilt. It screwed you up with the whole Nathan incident. Don't let it screw you up now." She puts her forehead against mine. "You don't deserve to be raped or threatened or have mean things posted about you or purposely hurt for any reason. Nobody does." She squeezes my hands. "Understand?"

I don't answer.

"Madison?"

I nod.

She sits back. "Now is not the time for guilt," she continues. "Now is the time for righteous anger. Calvin Westfall is a jerk of epic proportions. He treated you like crap in the relationship. He lied to you. He made you feel stupid for wanting to go after your dreams. He hurt you physically. He is the one that should feel guilty."

She's right. I know she's right. A tiny spark of anger toward him ignites inside me. I'm still really angry with myself, but I think Nathan's right that I have to let it go and forgive myself. I do believe Cal had a right to be angry with me for dumping him the way I did, but he didn't have a right to post those pictures or hurt me.

He's gone over to the dark side. And that's not my fault. He didn't have to lie to me or say those crude things about me to his friends either—that was before. And I sure didn't have anything to do with his selling drugs, because I never pressured him about taking me out or buying me things. I'm scowling as I think about these things, and I look over at Sophie who's grinning.

"There you go. Now, let's lay down some wrath."

Chapter Twenty-six

*G*od's timing is so perfect. The sermon on Sunday is about how we can't earn our salvation. We are always going to be sinful. Striving to be *good*, we'll fail every time. Shame and guilt are powerful weapons of the enemy that keep us looking at ourselves and our failures instead of fixing our eyes on Jesus. My eyes fill with tears, and I slip out of the sanctuary and find an empty classroom. What was I thinking? I couldn't *fix* what I did by staying with Cal—so sleeping with him would be *okay.* There's no way to *fix* it except to truly repent. I'm a big slobbering mess as I pray and thank Him that He went to the cross so He could forgive me.

I'm *not* worthy. But that's the point. No one is.

Still on a high of thankfulness, I do my research that afternoon. Class times. Prices. I even call Ms. Turpin just to be sure. Just to ask the question that I'm afraid to know the answer to.

Our doubts are traitors and make us lose the good we oft might win, by fearing to attempt. I will be brave. I will trust God for the outcome.

I'm in the hallway between the bathroom and my bedroom when she calls back, and my knees give out. I slide to the floor, take a deep breath, and answer. My explanation why I called starts weak but finishes strong.

"We'll have to start you out in the Intermediate classes," she tells me. "If you work hard, we should be able to bump you up to your own age group after six weeks or so."

"But I want to be in the Advanced Classes. It says they're for serious students that want to train five and six days a week. I'm a serious student. I want to try out for Company Two next May."

There's a pause. "Oh." I'm afraid she's going to say the same thing

Celeste said. "Okay. Based on your audition, I suppose I could let you in Level Four. I didn't realize how serious you were. Megan said you weren't going to take classes."

"Well, I'm not sure I can afford it. Is there any kind of discount for students paying for themselves?"

"I could give you a discount if you can teach a couple of classes for me. You're so good with the little ones."

"Thank you. That means a lot to me."

"I don't care how it makes you feel. I only care about how it makes you perform. We aren't like most studios in the area. We demand a lot."

"I know. I'm willing to work hard."

"Then I expect to see you tomorrow in class. Come at four to fill out paperwork. You're aware of our dress code?"

"Yes ma'am." Now is not the time for chickens. "Ms. Turpin?"

"Yes?"

"Celeste Peterson said that I was too tall and broad for the company. She said they only take a certain type. Is that true? Am I never going to fit into the company, no matter how hard I work?"

"It is true that a certain body type is preferred. But excellence trumps body type. We have several girls in the company right now who are about your size. They are often placed in the back in group numbers for aesthetic reasons, but they're there. We need a diverse group to be able to pull off such diverse productions."

I lean my head back on the wall. "Ms. Turpin?"

"Yes?"

"Do you think I have a chance?" I hold my breath.

"Madison, if you put as much of yourself into your classes as you do into your performance, I think you'll have a very good chance."

I feel all melty like warm ice cream. "Thank you. I'll see you tomorrow."

I call Abdulla at the Pansy and explain about having to leave early tomorrow. I also explain that I'll have to leave early on Monday, Tuesday, and Friday now to make it to class on time. I can still work until four-thirty on Wednesday and Thursday. But no more Friday nights or Saturday days either—I'll have to teach after morning classes on Saturday. He's not thrilled.

"You're going to have to work this out with Laurie," he says. "You're already scheduled for the next two weeks the old way. And I thought you had some kind of dance class at school on your short days, what are you doing about that?"

"I haven't exactly figured that out yet."

I call Laurie, and she's okay with the change because it gives her more hours. She's saving for college.

Then I email Ms. Vaughan about dance team. I don't have her phone number—not that I want to hear the disappointment in her voice. I won't have dance class on Thursday and most of our basketball games are on Thursday, but three are on Tuesday and two on Friday. And I can't make it to any of the team practices now, so I have to quit. I hate to do it because I know she counts on me, but I'm sure Chloe can take over.

When my parents get home from their trip, I wait until they are unpacked, relaxed, and having a glass of wine after dinner before I descend on them. I sit on the couch next to Mom and ask my dad to pause the TV.

"I have something to say, and it's probably going to come as a surprise, but I want you to hear me out." I have their full attention. They look a little scared. Maybe they think that I'm about to announce that I'm pregnant or something.

"I would like to start in the Advanced Level program at the City Ballet Studio tomorrow. It's very expensive, but I'm willing to pay for it myself. And Ms. Turpin said she could give me a discount for teaching some classes." They are both frowning, but I press on. I hand them each a copy of the class schedule with the cost written across the top. "I need to have that kind of daily training to prepare for auditions for the company in May."

Still, they don't say anything, but they are looking at the papers. Mom's face is scrunching up in a big frown.

"I want to audition for the company, and if I make it, great, but if I don't, I'd like to continue with classes and try out again."

My mom's eyes widen. "How are you going to do that and go to college too? What about teaching?"

I swallow hard and look her straight in the eye. "I've decided not to teach school. If I make it into the company, then I can go to Bellmeade—part time—if you're willing to help me pay for it." I explain about the program. "If I don't make it, I can begin General Studies classes at Bellmeade while I continue with training. If you're not willing to pay for college either because of the dance major, I'll pay for it myself somehow—maybe by working at the Pansy, maybe by teaching dance, maybe both."

My mom crosses her arms and leans back against the couch. "This is about that boy, isn't it? You don't want to go to UT because he's there. There are other schools with good teaching programs. You could go to Middle Tennessee. Then you could do some of your hands-on stuff at my school. Sophie is—"

"Mom. I don't want to be a teacher. I want to dance in a professional company."

"No. Absolutely not. Dance is a hobby, not a career. You can't make a living like that. It has no security." She looks at my dad. "Tell her."

My dad sets his wine glass down on the end table and sits up a little straighter in his recliner.

Before he can say anything, I say, "Kayleigh didn't figure out what she wanted to do until now. And it was breaking her heart and causing problems in her marriage when she and Derrick couldn't agree about it. I know you really wanted me to be a teacher, but if I do that, by the time I graduate, I doubt I'll be in the kind of shape I need to be in to be in a professional company, and maybe I'll be too old anyway. Because I want to teach dance too, and I want to get married someday, of course, and have kids. If I have to wait four years to start living my dreams, I'm just afraid I'll get distracted by...well, life, and end up settling."

I'm kind of out of breath from all that. My dad's frown has changed to an amused grin. He looks at my mom, but she is stone-faced.

He takes a deep breath and nods thoughtfully. "I can see you've given this a lot of thought."

"Yes."

"Of course, we want you to go for your dreams. But being a professional dancer doesn't pay very well and neither does teaching dance. You know I did Miss Gena's taxes."

I nod. "I also know you said every year, 'This woman must really love what she does in order to do it for so little return on her time.'"

He grins. "I guess I did."

"I'm willing to be a starving artist. I love dance enough."

My mom pipes up then. "What if you have an injury? What if the company folds?"

"Can't I cross that bridge when I get to it?"

"What about dance team?" she asks.

"I have to quit. There's no other way."

"And you're okay with that?" my dad asks. "I thought you loved dance team."

"I do, but I love ballet more. I won't be ready for auditions if I don't have that level of commitment." I nod at the schedule in his hand. "Ms. Turpin said I can start tomorrow."

"And your job? How are you going to keep up with your schoolwork, work every day, and go to class every evening?" My dad is frowning again.

"I've already talked to Abdulla. And Laurie's agreed to work the long days I can't. There's no hour requirement for C.E. If it gets to be too much, I'll cut back. But my class load is really light. My B- in Pre-Calculus was my lowest grade last semester and I managed *Nutcracker* rehearsals." I look back and forth between them hopefully, expectantly.

My mom looks at my dad like he's crazy. "Are you seriously considering letting her do this? I can't... It's not... No. Just no." She stomps off to their bedroom and shuts herself in.

"I don't want to disappoint her, but this is my life, and I have to choose the path that's best for me."

Finally.

This choice came through a hard lesson, and I won't back down.

"If you say no, I'll just pay for it myself and do it anyway. I'm almost eighteen." Didn't mean to play Sophie's trump card, but there it is.

He sighs. "I'll go talk to her."

He's on my side!

I pace the living room for a while as I wait; then settle on the couch. Resigned. *Doing it on my own—I can't even imagine.* I would, though. I'd have to. Like Nathan said, I know what I want, and now I have to figure out how to get it.

Twenty minutes pass before they come back.

They look at each other for a long minute and then back at me. I can't read their expressions. "Okay," my dad says finally.

I jump up from the couch. "Okay? I can do it?"

"Yes. And we'll pay for the classes, but you have to pay for your gas and car maintenance. We'll also pay for Bellmeade, with the stipulation that you to have a business minor, to help with your dance studio, or—" He looks at Mom, who is still not smiling. "Whatever obstacles come up."

I hug them both and thank them. "You are the best parents —ever!"

And I was so scared to tell them.

For the first time in months, I sleep like the dead.

Calvin deleted the pictures he posted, but Joey re-posted them, so they made the rounds with a whole new following. I text Cal to say that is just as bad and he better get Joey to delete them, or I'm posting about what he did to me. After some time, I check and they're gone, but I'm afraid the damage is already done.

When I walk to homeroom on Monday, I know it is.

There are stares and whispers. Suddenly, the band geek turned dance team captain that no one ever really noticed before is getting whistles and lewd comments from half the guys in school. Sophie catches up to me when I'm almost there, walking beside me like a sentinel, glaring at anyone that dares to say anything. I'm sure my face is bright red by the time I make it to the classroom.

She even walks me to my seat and stands beside me protectively. "We've got to post the pictures I took," she says. "Everyone feels sorry for that monster."

"I don't know. It'll die down faster if we don't."

Ken walks in and smiles at me, but his smile disappears when he sees Sophie's face.

"You are going to post that you did not sleep with Madison on every form of media you use," she tells him.

"No one thinks we slept together. If we had, she wouldn't have moved on to Lester." He says this to me as if I've missed out.

"Chloe is my friend. I know better than to sleep with you," I say. "How would you like me to tell everyone what I know about that?"

"You've got dirt on him and didn't tell me?" Sophie asks.

"It's not mine to tell," I explain. "But I will if I have to," I add.

"Fine." Ken whips out his phone and types furiously. He looks victorious when he's finished. "There. Reputation restored."

Sophie takes out her phone to check what he wrote, but the bell rings and she has to put it away.

"What did you say?" I ask him.

He leans in close, flashing that knock out smile. "I said, 'Too bad I didn't get to finish what I started with Madison. She is fine.'"

"Gee thanks. That'll help a lot." I turn back around in my seat. I guess I shouldn't have expected anything more gentlemanly from a guy willing to take advantage of a drunk girl.

"How about it?" He says over my shoulder into my ear. "You want to go out with me this weekend?"

"I'm not interested in finishing anything with you except this conversation."

Even Kendra has something to say when she slips into her desk in front of me, but it's not the pity that I expect, or the disgust from my horrible behavior. She shakes her head. "I am so glad you broke up with that jerk."

"Yeah. Dodged the bullet there." Although it did graze me pretty painfully, but she doesn't have to know the gory details.

"You sure did. If he's this mean to you because you broke up with him…well, good riddance!"

I just nod. I'm kind of in awe of her loyalty. We were best friends in second grade, but that was a long time ago.

"Your real friends know that stuff's not true." She gets out her notebook then turns back around and adds, "I know we're not that close anymore, but if you need anyone to talk to, I'm here." She has a Bible verse across the top of her notebook: Philippians 4:8.

"Thanks, Kendra. You're a good friend. What's that verse? I forgot."

"Whatever is true, whatever is noble, whatever is right, whatever is pure, whatever is lovely, whatever is admirable—if anything is excellent or praiseworthy—think about such things."

"Oh, yeah. I used to know that by heart, too."

"It's my go-to verse. I mean, it reminds me not to gossip or watch things or read things I shouldn't. It keeps me focused on Christ." I return her smile, and she turns back around.

I swallow hard. *Scripture.* If I had been memorizing scripture instead of Shakespeare, maybe I could have heard what the Holy Spirit was trying to tell me.

I search the halls between classes for Chloe to tell her about dance team and finally spot her before English.

"Chloe, can I talk to you?"

"I don't really want to talk to you," she snaps. "I cannot believe you made out with him. What is wrong with you? Are you going to start dating him now? After what he did to me?"

"Of course not. And we didn't even—"

"What's your plan?" she cuts in. "You running against Lisa for Most Likely to Do It with Every Guy in School?"

That hurts coming from her. "I was drunk and stupid. I can't even tell you how much I regret it. I'm really sorry. That's not what I wanted to talk to you about anyway."

"Well, save it for practice." She walks away. "Maybe by then I'll be able to talk to you."

I guess some of my friends do believe it all.

I have butterflies in my stomach as I drive to work. Does Nathan regret being so nice to me? Is he going to *give me time*, whatever that means, again? I just want to go back to the easy way it was before Christmas, before I got off track.

When I come through the kitchen, Rick is in there. He comes behind me as I clock in and drapes an arm over my shoulder. Then his hand wanders down my back to my butt. I shove him away and slap his face.

His mouth is hanging open in surprise. "What was that for?"

"You knew I was drunk, and you were still going to take me to your room. If you ever touch me again, I will seriously damage your family plans."

I underestimated the power of righteous anger. It makes me feel strong and whatever the opposite of guilty is—blameless? Exonerated? I like it.

I look over to see if Abdulla saw. He did and is headed my way, but behind him Nathan is smiling.

Abdulla passes me and goes straight to Rick, getting right up in his face. "She is under age, and you are twenty-one and an assistant manager. Do you want to be brought up on charges of sexual harassment? If you ever touch an employee inappropriately again, you are fired. And that's your second strike." Abdulla storms out of the kitchen. I rush to help Laurie who's trying to handle the counter alone.

She gives me a grin and whispers, "Way to go. He is such a perv."

When my shift ends, I really want to talk to Nathan, but I have to run by the dancewear store for new tights and the appropriate color leotards, so I don't have time. I do slip over to the pizza making side to tell him.

"I talked to my parents." I can't help the huge smile on my face. "I start class today, in a few hours."

He looks up from his work. "Wow. It's nice to see that smile again. I'm glad things worked out."

"It wouldn't have happened without your encouragement, so, thanks."

He nods and sprinkles cheese on the pie he's making. "I was glad to see you stand up to Rick."

"Sophie is teaching me how to channel my righteous anger." I look around and pop a mushroom in my mouth. I don't know how I'm going to have time to eat today. I better start packing a dinner. "It's…liberating."

"Much healthier than guilt." He slides the tremendous spatula thingy under the finished pizza so he can put it in the oven.

I'm about to get in major trouble for being near the ovens. "I better go. Just wanted you to know."

"Okay. Have fun at practice."

"If I do, then I won't be working hard enough." I laugh and grab another mushroom for the road.

I'm so excited to be at my first dance class. And nervous. Megan walks in while I am tying my pointe shoes, and her face lights up.

"I thought you weren't going to do it," she says.

"We know what we are but know not what we may be." I look up, and she is frowning. "Sorry. I throw out Shakespeare quotes all the time. Better get used to it."

She sits next to me and pulls off her street shoes. "Okay. What's it mean?"

"I had given up on my dreams last time we spoke. But I have since realized that giving up is not an option. *I know what I am*—a pretty good dancer—*but know not what I may be*—a professional dancer. *If* I work my tail off." We both laugh.

The technique class is brutal. Beyond brutal. I'm not as good as the other students my age, but I'm close. I can get there. I think I did okay in the other classes. There are stares and whispers about the bruises on my arms. None of the girls come out and ask, not even Megan, but Ms. Turpin did when I filled out the paperwork. I just say there was an incident with an ex-boyfriend. Emphasis on the *ex*.

"I better not see fresh bruises anytime," she says.

"You won't."

I'll never allow myself to be treated like that again. And now that I've turned it over to God and trust He's forgiven me, I can finally forgive myself, too. I know now that I am complete because of my relationship with Christ. Nothing in this world, not dancing, or sex, or drinking, or having someone say he loves me, can ever fill up those empty places like He does.

Chapter Twenty-seven

Ms. Vaughan is curt in her email response, but she tells me to come to rehearsal when I can on Thursday to tell everyone in person why I won't be there anymore. I'm dreading it all day. Especially talking to Chloe.

I get to the school at five-fifteen, when it's almost over. It's strangely quiet in the halls. Usually, the music can be heard all the way down the hall. I see Maura, a freshman, sitting outside the practice room. I wave as I approach, but she darts into the room like a startled rabbit.

When I walk into the room they shout, "Surprise!"

It's a goodbye party. For me.

Surprised? Shocked is more like it. I was expecting everyone to be mad at me. I was expecting them to feel hurt and betrayed for me to leave with no warning, but here they are with cake instead.

Ms. Vaughan comes over and hugs me. "Madison, we all want you to know how much we've appreciated your hard work running the practices, choreographing the numbers, and motivating everyone. We are so proud that you are following your dream to be a professional dancer and want to wish you the best of luck."

"Even though you don't need it," Chloe says and hands me a knife. "Cut the cake and make a wish."

It's chocolate with marshmallow icing which sticks to the knife. My wish is that leaving them is worth the sacrifice.

Everyone is standing around eating cake when Chloe comes over to me. "I'm sorry I got mad Monday. A little residual jealousy I guess."

"It's okay. I don't know what I was thinking. I wasn't thinking really." I lick the icing off my fork and lower my voice. "And I had no idea alcohol makes you so…" I whisper, my face gets hot.

She laughs. "Turned on? Might want to remember that, for next time."

"No way. No next time for me."

She scrapes her plate with her fork, getting the last of the creamy, marshmallowy goodness. "Think of us slaving away in our boring college classes when you're performing *Swan Lake* or whatever."

"I've got a lot of work to do before I audition. I may not make it. And I'll be taking classes part-time at Bellmeade next fall even if I do."

"You'll make it. And I will buy season tickets next year so I can see you." She hugs me. "You're gonna be great."

During the next three weeks with school and classes and work, I feel like I'm alone all the time. But not lonely. It's weird to me now how lonely I was when Cal left for college. How I longed for him. It was pitiful. How could I not have seen how pathetic I was? When people say love is blind, they really mean infatuation is obsessive and too stupid to see what's right in front of its face.

Or maybe, because we want love so much, we can't see the lies we tell ourselves.

My happily ever after isn't dependent on a romantic relationship. It *is* dependent on me going after my dreams and not settling. And believing that God is already directing my path, so I don't have to worry or beg for signs. It was worrying and trying to force an outcome that would please other people that got me off track.

I tear down all the Shakespeare quotes from my wall and print out some encouraging Bible verses instead, like Philippians 4:8 and this one from Colossians 2:8: "See to it that no one takes you captive through hollow and deceptive philosophy, which depends on human tradition and the elemental spiritual forces of this world rather than on Christ." Putting these in my head and heart will help me keep focused on what's truly important.

On Saturday night three weeks later, I have to close, and Nathan is working for Scott, so he's here too. We haven't had a chance to really talk this whole month, and I'm not sure if that was his choice or just circumstances. I'm dying to tell him about the dance team party and how classes are going, but maybe he doesn't want to be friends. Maybe he wants to go back to being…whatever we were.

"After work, can we talk?" he says, as he passes me at the dishwasher.

"Sure," I tell him, but then I don't see him again, and after Abdulla locks us in to clean, I see that he's already clocked out.

I'm disappointed as I walk to my car, but his car is next to mine in the parking lot. I look up on the roof and grin. There's smoke coming from it. I throw my purse in my car and meet him up there.

He's sitting in one of the chairs beside the little grill with the broken legs warming his hands over it. He has cleaned and dried off the other chair.

"I thought you said next time we talked, you wanted it to be inside," I say as I sit.

"Too many ears inside," he says. "Besides, it's not so bad with a fire."

I shiver and go to my knees to be closer to it. "If you say so."

"How are things going?" he asks.

All the things I've been longing to tell him pour out of me in a big rush. His eyes are sparkling as he listens. As I talk, I think that must be the reason I love to talk to him. He is the best listener I've ever known. When I finish, he moves down to his knees, too, to be closer to the warm coals.

"What did you want to talk about?" I ask.

His face turns serious. "There's something I've been wanting to tell you."

Uh-oh, here it comes. The "it's better if we're not friends" speech. My stomach does a back handspring, and I look away from his big brown eyes. I draw circles with my finger in the gravel dust.

He takes a big breath. "When I first started working here, I wasn't thrilled when I found out I'd be seeing you every day. I guess I still had some bad feelings about what happened, even though I told you I didn't."

I feel the tears coming and take a deep breath to hold them back.

He sits in the chair and runs his hands through his hair. "Do you want to hear this? Because I'd understand if you don't. I've been trying to give you some time, but I felt like this needed to be said. Especially after some of the things you said that night after the party. I just wanted to put it out there. We don't have to do anything about it."

Do anything about it? I'm confused. "I'm not sure what you mean, but if you're about to tell me that you don't want to be friends with me anymore…I…I don't…" I can't finish the sentence. I get up and get the sleeping bag out of the bag and spread it out as close to the grill as I dare and lie down. It's a clear night, and I figure I can handle what he's going to say better if I'm looking at the stars instead of him.

He comes and lies beside me, leaving about a foot between us.

"I wasn't going to say that," he says and relief floods my heart. "Since ninth grade I've dated five or six different girls, but none of the relationships lasted very long. I think I've been comparing them to what we had.

"I never blamed you for what happened. You had just said the week before how you wished we were old enough to drive so we could go on real dates. And then I told you I loved you, and you didn't say it back. I thought I rushed you and scared you off, so when the opportunity to go on a real date with an older guy came along, you took it.

"The reason I fell in love with you, if it was love at fourteen, was because of the way we could talk, always, about anything. And I've never had that with anyone else since."

He tries to put his hands behind his head, but he nearly hits me with his elbow, so he puts them back down. I lie perfectly still, afraid that any movement will keep him from saying these wondrous things.

"When we started working together, I thought it had been too long, and we had changed too much for that connection to still be there. I don't know about you, but for me, it felt like we just picked up where we left off."

I dare to turn my head and look at him and smile. It must

encourage him because he says, "You just went through a lot and probably shouldn't jump right into another relationship, so I just want you to know that I'm here when you're ready. If you want."

I look back at the stars, and it hurts a lot to do it, but I say, "I'm not good enough for you, Nathan. I wish I was, but I know I'm not. You deserve so much better than me."

"I think I can figure out what is or isn't good for me."

For a moment, I can only hear my heart pounding in my ears and see the tiny clouds our breaths create. *Could he really, truly want—me?*

"Is that your only objection, or are you not interested and trying to let me down easy? Or did you just want to stay friends?"

I'm feeling a little overwhelmed, my eyes fill, and my heart is racing. I don't say anything. I'm hardly breathing.

"I have a Shakespeare quote for you," he says. "No more be grieved at that which thou hast done. Roses have thorns, and silver fountains mud. Clouds and eclipses stain both moon and sun. And loathsome canker lives in sweetest bud."

The joy of this beautiful night, lying next to this beautiful boy, who has just bared his beautiful heart to me, warms me as if we are in the sun on a summer day.

I tell him my side. "When I first met Calvin, it was right after the necklace incident. Sophie convinced me that I needed to let go of my feelings for you. Calvin and I could talk easily, at first, it was really more like debates, but I confused it for what we had, because I so desperately wanted to have that again." I dare to peek at him. He's smiling.

"I convinced myself of a lot of things that weren't true." And I know that he knows that I'm talking about my love for Calvin and my belief that I had to give up my dreams because I had sex with him, and my recent shameful behavior as some sort of proof that I shouldn't forgive myself. I know he knows because he does get me. Like no one else.

"That day, under the bleachers, I always regretted not saying it back to you. Because I did love you. I don't think I ever stopped. Being with you isn't jumping into a new relationship. Our relationship has been here all along. And I think… No, I *know* I have the perspective now to understand it for what it is."

He puts his cold hand over mine. "You want to go to church with me tomorrow?"

"I'd like that."

The stars are winking at me as if a thousand angels are saying, "That's it. *Now* you're reading the signs."

Cal was right about one thing: real life isn't Shakespeare. But sometimes, it's just as beautiful.

1. Do you surround yourself with people that help you or hinder you in your walk with God? Do you sometimes feel that the actions of others influence you to lower your standards?
2. Madison tried to hold firm to the biblical standard of not having sex before marriage. She had a friend to help hold her accountable. But increasingly, she allowed herself to cross a line with physical intimacy. How far is too far, in your opinion, when it comes to sexual purity? Is it okay to cross those lines if you want to marry the person?
3. Do you think it's biblical to believe all sin sends you to hell like Sophie's parents? Can we earn our salvation through "good" behavior? What role does repentance play in our salvation? On the other side of that, do you think some people give themselves a free pass to sin, counting on God's forgiveness? What do you think unrepentant sin (or living in sin because "everyone else does it") does to your relationship with God?
4. Often when we are in a relationship, we have trouble having a clear perspective. Have your friends ever told you that you aren't acting like yourself when you're around someone you're dating? Did you act differently because you were afraid of losing the relationship? Should you have to act differently so someone will like you? From the other side of that equation, have you ever dated someone who acts differently when you're alone together than when you're with others?
5. Have you ever excused abusive behavior, whether physical or emotional, because you didn't think it would happen

again, or convinced yourself it wasn't a big deal? Did you ever let the person's cutting words convince you that you deserved it?

6. Do you think it's biblical to ask God to give you a sign? Do you ever think about God's will for your life? God's will is for us to love Him with all our heart and soul and love others as much as we love ourselves. How does following God's will and having free will work together? Do you think sin is outside of God's will for us? Do you think God would ever give you a sign (or open a door for you) that would point you to sin?

7. What do you think is the best way to open yourself up to hear the Holy Spirit when you are struggling to make a decision?

For more biblical reflections on these topics, get the companion Bible study/devotional *Whatever is True* by Stephanie Cardel, also from WordCrafts Press. Available wherever books are sold online.

Acknowledgements

*L*ike most authors, my road to publication has been very long, and many people helped me along the way and have helped in the months leading up to publication. I couldn't possibly name them all. *Thank you all so much!*

I am so grateful to all the critique partners I've had—even if they didn't critique this book. Each one helped me grow as a writer, especially Janelle Leonard, Kristy Boyce, Sharon Cameron, Cindy Phiffer (and the Ladies at Table), and Helene Dunbar. I am grateful to the Midsouth SCBWI, Jillian Boehme and her Miss Snark's First Victim blog contest (now archived) that helped me get my first agent. (Jillian is now a friend and client who also critiqued this new version for me along with her daughter—thanks, Jill and Molly!) Many thanks to my first agent, Nicole Payne, who tried to sell the secular version of this book and believed in the heart of this story. I'm also very grateful to all the authors and agents at Golden Wheat Literary, especially Jessica Schmeidler—you taught me so much. But I couldn't have made it to publication without the support and feedback of my dear family, especially Rachel and Elle (also writers) and the love and patience of my sweet husband Dean, who always supported my dreams—even before we were married. Many thanks to Mike Parker and WordCrafts Press for agreeing that the world needed Maddy's story. And finally, many thanks to Anna Hester, the talented artist that designed the cover. It's just what I wanted.

Stephanie Cardel is the founder of Lighthouse Literary Agency. She lives on a farm in middle Tennessee with her husband and their goldendoodle. They have three grown children and five precious grandchildren.

She led VBS and wrote and directed Christmas plays at her church when her children were young. Then she turned to the women's ministry and was active planning events and leading Bible studies, which she continues to do. She had the pleasure of being on the crew of three faith-based films and a Christmas movie and even had a small part in three of them.

She taught abstinence-based sex education in the public schools for five years. She co-wrote a Christian advice column on the *Daughter of Delight* website for two years, which is still available in the archives. She is a member of the MidSouth SCBWI and the ACFW.

This Isn't Shakespeare is her debut novel.

Connect with Stephanie online at:

www.stephaniecardel.com

Also Available From

WORDCRAFTS PRESS

Along the Forgotten Coast
by Jennifer Odom

Paint Me Fearless
by Hallie Lee

Yeah, But I Didn't
by Ann Swann

Road Trip
by Marian Rizzo & Mario Villella

27 Words
by KL Palmer

www.WordCrafts.net